W9-DFE-595

STOLEN STORIES

BOOKS BY STEVE KATZ

The Exagggerations of Peter Prince
Creamy and Delicious
Posh
Saw
Cheyenne River Wild Track
The Lestriad
The Weight of Antony
Moving Parts
Wier & Pouce

Steve Katz

STOLEN STORIES

FICTION COLLECTIVE

NEW YORK

FIRST EDITION

Library of Congress Cataloging-in-Publication Data

Katz, Steve, 1935-
   Stolen stories.

   I. Title.
PS3561.A77487   1984   813'.54   83-27410
ISBN 0-914590-84-7
ISBN 0-914590-85-5   paper

Grateful acknowledgment is made to the following magazines and anthologies in
which these stories first appeared: *Fiction* for "The Perfect Life"; *American Review*
for "Friendship"; *Lillabulero* for "One on One"; *Seattle Review* for "Mongolian
Whiskey"; *Seems* for "Two Seaside Yarns" and "Made of Wax"; *Statements 2* for
"Two Seaside Yarns"; *Center* for "Two Essays" and "on SELF KNOWLEDGE"; *Oyez* for
"Smooth"; *Tri-Quarterly* for "Three Essays"; *Epoch* for "Three Essays" and
"Bumpkin"; *Statements* for "Death of the Band"; and *The Cornell Review* for "The
Stolen Stories."

Published by the Fiction Collective with assistance from the National Endowment for
the Arts and the New York State Council on the Arts, and with the cooperation of
Brooklyn College, Teachers & Writers Collaborative, and Illinois State University.

Typeset by Open Studio, Ltd., in Rhinebeck, New York, a non-profit facility for
writers, artists and independent literary publishers, supported in part by grants from
the New York State Council on the Arts.

Manufactured in the United States of America.

Text design: McPherson & Company
Cover and jacket design: Sara Eisenman
Back jacket and cover photograph: Reg Saner
Front jacket and cover photograph: Courtesy of Istvan Kottki

CONTENTS

The Perfect Life   9

Friendship   17

One on One   27

Mongolian Whiskey   35

Two Seaside Yarns   53

Two Essays   59

Smooth   65

Three Essays   77

Death of the Band   83

Bumpkin   99

Made of Wax   103

on Self Knowledge   119

The Stolen Stories   123

STOLEN STORIES

THE PERFECT LIFE

THE PERFECT LIFE

Something I have done has made me famous, but I can't remember what it is. This belt-buckle is the trophy that demonstrates what I say is true. One of those silver buckles with a portrait of myself in profile embossed on the face. Etched very lightly on my cheek is a picture of half the earth seen from the arctic. The major ports are indicated by the tiniest emeralds and the capitals of countries by chiplets of turquoise. Unfortunately I have no record of the events leading up to the presentation of this buckle, but that no one has asked for it back should be proof enough that my achievements were solid. I don't intend to let them have it back.

Around the perimeter of my arctic projection some little foliage develops every Spring and browns away each Fall. If I put my ear to the buckle I hear a faint whistle, like a cardinal, but so faraway. You, from the shoulders up, is the image engraved on my eye. You wear a collar of microscopic opals. What the artist has captured is Your subtle energy. Your eyes are half closed, Your lips are slightly puckered; I can actually feel them as a light, reassuring scratch when I run my finger over my eye on the face of my buckle.

Conclusions from my simplest research are inscribed on the uneven lines radiating from my mouth. Those words didn't make me famous. Mankind doesn't value them. No one has heard of them. Not only have they been ignored, but many of the inscriptions are misquotes. Words were misspelled.

Punctuation in shambles. In fact, the whole buckle is clumsily done. It's a failure. If I were still famous I would insist it be remade, according to my own design; but now I don't care, because right now I am enjoying that which my admirers call The Perfect Life.

What they call The Perfect Life I know simply as experience limited to the sense of smell. I will explain what I mean by giving the following example, which I call A VISIT FROM YOU:

Whiff of oranges at the door and I know it's You. You come in as if camomile. I will let no one else interrupt my work. You embrace me like a closet of herbs—thyme of the negligee, tarragon in loose cotton pants, fresh basil of the underclothes, rosemary sweaters, denim oregano. From behind Uou touch my cheek: lavender, lemon-flower water on the palms of Your hands.

"You smell like the woods," You say. "I love ferniness. All my other men smell like aluminum."

I close the whiff of ink in my book. Your hand sniffs down my back and I raise up. My tongue nicks the cinnamon of Your throat. My snout dives into your breasts. "Bayberry on the right," I say. "And Japanese sesame oil on the left."

Your sniffer is in my hair. "Crushed almonds," You whisper. "Thank you."

"What's to thank?" say I. I snort the mintiness of your breath and drop to Your wild bellybutton garlic. You slip out of your pants.

"Does anything have to mean something?" You ask.

"Sure." I glide my nose down the light sarsaparilla of Your thighs, Your knee-creases thick with anise.

I feel heat from Your nostrils on my backbone as You lightly touch down on each vertebra: "Fresh-cut black locust, the oak, sugar maple, mountain ash." You have such sensitivity. "Cedar. Wet cedar shakes," You shout when You reach the base of my spine. I roll over and hurl my nose into your ripe peach and You encourage the banana-oil.

"Bananas and horses and low tide," You say. "All at once."

Outside the bikers kick over all at once. The room fills with exhaust. We rub wrinkled noses and get up.

"We almost forgot," You say.

"Forgot what?" The Perfect Life has been interrupted.

"He gets in in a few hours. We have to meet Him."

"Is She on the same flight?"

"Tomorrow morning She arrives."

If I had the services at my command that I did when my popularity was peaking I would meet Him at the airport in a chauffeured limo; but as it stands right now we're hitching to the airport. Me and You.

Chaos at Pan-Am. A 707 tilted over on one crumpled wing, surrounded by ambulances and fire-engines. The runway covered with foam, passengers sliding down chutes, running through the foam like screaming cloud-creatures, leaving a trail of hand- luggage behind. At gate 43 people are terrified, wringing their hands, looking for their aging grandmothers.

"Luckeeee," says a stewardess to a ticket agent. "Only one casualty." Survivors stagger through the gate. You grab me by the elbow, expecting the worst. An old man, carrying an ancient Gladstone bag, approaches You. "Would you be interested in a battery-powered watch?" He stumbles down the corridor without waiting for an answer.

By now We know who the one casualty is. We check the passenger list just to be sure. His name is on it, the name He uses. You wait outside the door of the infirmary as I go in to see what's left of Him. His body lies on a rolling table in the corridor. He is dead alright. Just as I get there He sits up. "I don't think we blew it. I think we did good," He says. "But they want exact change on these buses." Before He lies down forever He places three small packets in my hand. I slip them into my pocket as an attendant comes around the corner. "Do you know this man?" he asks. "I thought I did," I say, "but it's not the one." He watches me with suspicion as I leave the building. We don't dare look for His luggage. We spend all our money on the bus back to the city.

I start to sneeze when We get to my place, and You have a fit of trembling at the table. I lay the three carefully wrapped packets in front of You. You push them away. "It wasn't worth it," You say. I slump over. His death is on us like a crippling disease. I wish it were still in my power to reverse the course of human events.

We are back at the airport on the next morning expecting Her arrival. In the old days I would have brought the band, or an entire film crew. Her arrival is an event, this time uneventful. She wears a long knit coat, and She has shaved her head. The shape of her skull is elegant and feminine. You two embrace immediately, but I see Her searching for Him over your shoulder. You separate, and She starts to look around as if lost. I don't know how to begin to ask Her to lend us some money. I place His three small packets in Her hand, and She understands. She stares at them a moment and then lets out a long thin sigh that colors the air around us violet. Every moment has become serious. I would like to be able to do a thing that would start us moving again towards The Perfect Life. We need some money. She tosses the three packets into a large trash barrel, where they begin to burn with a greenish flame that seems like the end of something. Her sad, dim, brave smile is thrilling.

"You don't have to cry on my account."

I'm not crying. "What was in those packets?" I ask.

"That's all over," she says. "We lived that way in the sixties. I expected this to happen some day. I was ready." She is standing in a piss-yellow light. "I suppose that now I'll have to start to grow up. But don't cry on my account."

I see now that She isn't looking at my face, but at my belt buckle. I take it off to examine it myself. She is right. There is a perfect tear formed on top of the eye on my face embossed there. What a mistake. In that tear I see Your face magnified, pucker widening to a smile, bunching back to a pucker again. Your jaws are moving. You are chewing bubble gum, and out of Your pucker a pink bubble starts to grow, at first just as big as the tiny tip of Your tongue, then it slowly fills with Your perfect breath.

This could be a disaster. This could be bad timing. The bubble is visible to the naked eye. It covers my whole embossed face, then the expanse of my whole buckle, obscuring this trophy. It's so unreal. The bubble is still expanding. Suddenly I begin to hear the voices inside that bubble. I don't believe it at first but then I figure out that certain voices must have been trapped in there when my buckle was originally fabricated. Another blunder for them. Originally the voices were probably supposed to broadcast words of praise for me to hear, but they had been fixed at such a low volume that I never really got to hear them, not until now as they are amplified by the bubble growing from Your lips:

"The concerts are over." "Buy us some beer." "We aren't moving." "Don't ruin those tickets." "Stay a week, or a month." "Stay till October." "Are there some messages?" "It doesn't work." "How about the booze?" "Is this a trap?" "Take your medicine." "I'll make the time." "What's the catch?" "We aren't moving." "Get us a broom." "Don't forget to write." "Which is the entrance?" "We aren't moving." "Do you feel sick?" "You are very interesting." "Let's get started." "Go to bed." "We aren't moving." "I live in a tent." "Turn her loose."

FRIENDSHIP

FRIENDSHIP

My friend Sadie was a closet cannibal and that was why I introduced her to Herman in the first place. At the time I thought it was best for people to get these propensities out in the open, at least on some level. Express yourself. Let it all hang out. I thought Herman might do that for her because among all my friends he was the one who tended to be most willing, even driven, to sacrifice himself.

"It's the 'iffiness' of this life we lead," Sadie once confided to me. "It's not even the old-fashioned ennui. That would seem better than this blank anxiety that we always feel. It's not as simple as plain boredom." Sadie pushed her long black hair back from her eyes. Those eyes had an enticing grey-green clarity, cat-like, startling. "It's this edginess, and what's worse, a fear of losing the edge because then you'd have nothing. You know what I mean."

"It's a long down drag, Sadie, but you've got to make the best of it, whatever." I've always believed that between friends a little banality is like a shot in the arm.

"Anthony, it's a total disaster. I'd rather live in some primitive society, in New Guinea, in a jungle, where my life was directed with certainty by some explicit rituals that defined the parameters of knowing the world, for myself and for everyone around me. Then there'd be no question of what to do. But we have all this choice. We live in this big city of feasts, and so you can never decide what's worth doing."

"Sadie, we can't go back to the dark ages."

"If I didn't have my bodily functions: eating, getting up, sleeping, shitting, fucking; if I didn't menstruate I'd never know when to do anything. I'm like a dung beetle pushing around a crappy little ball of time. Not even that beetle can feel what I feel. How do you get through a month without menstruating?"

"Your problem is twofold, Sadie: you've got too much intelligence, and you're genuinely ridiculous. Just relax. Let it flow."

"I know it," she said. She leaned over to kiss me. Sadie and I had a thing going, a fucking thing that happened two or three times a month. I can't stand it any more than that. She bites me so hard she sometimes draws blood. When she comes, she comes with her teeth clamped into my shoulder so deep that I start to scream. I hate it, but I like it too because she's my friend. When I leave her my body looks like one of those early paintings by Larry Poons, full of lozenge shaped bruises. I think when I finally close my art gallery I'll auction off my body as the last work of art. I never liked it in the first place. Gloria, my girl-friend, is a model. She never sees the bruises because with me she likes to pretend she is enormously fat and ashamed of her body. We make love in the dark and she has the soft slow style that I like best.

Herman moved in after seeing Sadie just a couple of times, and the change in her was almost immediate. I could see in her face that the potential of her life had expanded beyond her imagination. She forgot the whole line of bullshit she had been laying down for me about modern life and its general fucked-upness. Anthropology was her gig, and she started reading Levi-Strauss and Mircea Eliade again with a totally new set of eyes.

The change in Herman was slower, but I could see it happening to him too. He was growing, slowly pushing through his hang-ups. It's my biggest pleasure in life to get two of my friends together from different worlds, and to see them both begin to groove on each other. I used to think I loved art more than anything else in the world, but then it became my business. Now for me it's just another scam. It earns the bread and butter, such as it is. I realize now that what I really love is people. Friends. Keeping them happy.

"I wish I could thank you enough for introducing us. My whole life has changed," said Herman. "Sadie is the best thing that has happened to me in years; in fact, she's the only thing."

"Don't thank me," I said. I must admit I get a real glow from situations like this. "You're both friends of mine. I didn't do anything. Some day you'll find something to do for me."

"I hope so," Herman took my hand. His eyes were lit up like a fanatic's. "Her mind is so engaged. She has so much energy. She talks and I feel like I'm burning in the flame of her intellect. I haven't had so many thoughts since I was in college. I'm almost flattered to be allowed to listen to her."

"Don't underestimate yourself, Herman. Sadie's very bright and very articulate, but you've got a brilliant mind in your own way. She recognizes this in you."

Herman's grin was so wide he couldn't sip his espresso.

"What is it?" I asked.

He leaned towards me. "I didn't want to at first, but now I think I'll show you."

"What?"

Herman lifted his left pants leg to reveal a bandage on his calf. When he removed the bandage, I saw that a hunk of flesh was missing.

"How did that happen?"

"I gave it to her," he said, smiling even wider.

"You what?"

"I don't mind. She was hungry. She just wanted a taste."

"Wait a second. You mean you fed her from your own calf?" Although I mentioned when I started relating this anecdote that Sadie was a closet cannibal I must admit that I felt that analysis was just a figure of speech, meant symbolically or something, to help you get a quick fix on her. I never expected the cannibal to come out of the closet. I guess that's New York City. It pampers people to their extremes.

"This happened so naturally," Herman said. "The way

everything else happens between us. We had just made love. She said she was hungry and there wasn't a thing in the house. I sat up to try to think of something and the blanket fell off my leg. She looked at it. I looked at her. She looked into my eyes. It was understood. It wasn't one of those intellectual things, although our intellectual compatibility is a help. She keeps a paring knife in her night table drawer. First she cut off a little piece, held it in her mouth for the flavor, and swallowed it like an oyster. She looked so delighted I didn't believe it. I was flattered. I didn't even notice my pain. 'Take. Take some more,' I said. She took another hunk, and that was it. She broiled it. I figure all that muscle doesn't make any difference to me in my line of work."

He had a point there. Herman was a stamp dealer. I mean he was a heavyweight dealer in stamps. Better than $18,000 of philately passed through his store every week. He certainly didn't need muscle.

"You know," he went on. "If someone else did it I'd think it was weird, but I don't think it's weird because it's between me and her. Do you think it's weird?"

"If . . . if . . . if it's what the two of you want, Herman, who am I to judge? You're both my friends."

He looked so happy I felt like cupid.

For the two months I was in Germany I hardly thought about Sadie and Herman. Gloria came along with me, and between listening to her complaints about German food, and pushing my artists' work, I had plenty to think about. But the couple came to mind occasionally, as friends often do. I had two images of them that I could not reconcile. One was of this obsequiously happy couple, both of whom I loved, and the other was these two strangers performing a ritual I could never understand. You can bring friends together, I kept reminding myself, but you can't influence the way they're going to work out their relationship.

Gloria was getting even thinner, if you can imagine it, but at night she was into clomping around in some wooden shoes she had bought on a side trip to Sweden, and imitating the voice of an enormous hausfrau. She'd jump on top of me in bed and I'd pretend to be crushed. She did this in München and Köln, but she nearly flipped out in Hamburg and I had to send her back to the States.

I concentrated then on selling art. At this point in time the Germans have real avant-garde taste. Very analytical. Like my taste. They take it minimal, crisp, conceptual. That's what I've got in my shop so I do okay over there. I keep the paint squiggles on canvas, the bunch of junk welded together, all that vomit of the ego, out of my gallery. I've stayed away from figurative too, even though it sells. I hope before I have to peddle any of that I go out of business. Anyway, I go to Germany and get the Marks. With the dollar sinking that isn't bad business.

I went to visit Sadie once more after I got back. She was so effervescent, so gay, so untroubled when she answered the door that I hardly recognized her. She had chintzed up all her windows, covered her couch with an embroidered antimacassar, polished the ashtrays. It was unbelievable. It was strange. She kissed me lightly, a little tic, hardly the kind of wide-open sucking of my tongue she used once to threaten me. I sensed the thing we once had was probably over forever.

"You look so splendid, Sadie," I said.

"I am splendid," she replied.

I noticed another woman, a bull-dyke type, with a d.a. and baggy pants, eyeing me from the easy chair, over her copy of Steppenwolf. "That's sister Nathan," said Sadie. "She's an old friend."

"And Herman."

"He's here. He's here. He's been asking about you. You'll see him. First I'll make some tea."

I didn't like the way that sounded. Sadie always took forever to make tea. It was a production. I tried, without being too conspicuous, looking around the apartment for Herman, but he was not to be seen.

"Come on," she said, finally bringing the tea. "Herman talks about you all the time and he's just going to be so happy to see you."

She led me to a closet in the hall, and I had a chilling premonition of what would be in there. I felt like I had stepped into the Twilight Zone.

"Don't make any wise-ass remarks about praying mantises or whatever. This is something that happened between us. This is the way we like it," said Sadie, before she opened the door.

"You don't need to be defensive, Sadie," I reassured her. "Remember I was the one who introduced you in the first place."

There was such beatitude in Sadie's sudden smile, so much peace, that I felt I could allow her any transgression. "You're so great," she sang, and pulled open the closet door.

"What a treat to see you, Anthony. It's been months," said Herman. "So much has happened." I could see that. Herman was in the closet; at least, what remained of him. His carcass, carved up neatly, hung from coathangers, and was talking to me. "Isn't this great. I feel like a million dollars. Sadie's a terrific cook."

I didn't find the sight repulsive; in fact, if I remember at all what I felt it was a sense of utter absurdity. My own friends. For once I was at a loss for words.

"Have you been selling any stamps, Herman?"

"The business takes care of itself, Anthony. And if it doesn't, I've made enough money in my life. It's about time I started living."

"You said a mouthful, Herman." She had just cut the filets off of him, and had left most of the stuff around the vital organs. The bones were all there. She hadn't eaten the liver. She hadn't eaten the heart. I wouldn't have believed it if I hadn't seen it with my own eyes.

"It even feels good this way, Anthony. It's good for the head. It's relaxing. I'm conscious of so much more. I'd thank you again, but I don't want to sound insincere."

"It's okay, Herman. I only introduced you. I can't take credit for anything else." I started to close the closet. "I'll see you around."

"Anthony," said Herman, just before the door shut. "Will you do me a favor?"

I pulled the door open a little, "What?"

"Will you speak to my bookkeeper? I really like the guy."

"What'll I tell him?"

"I don't know. Make it up. Tell him philately isn't everything in life. Tell him to sell the one penny magenta and the tete-beche collection. Tell him to sell all the stamps and to go to the Seychelles Islands. Give him my regards. Give him a bonus."

"I'll do that, Herman," I said, and finally closed the door.

Sadie had the tea poured in the other room. "That's heavy," I said to her.

She turned on me, obviously expecting my strong reaction. "Look. Different people work out different trips." A look passed over her face so dark it reminded me of the Sadie I once knew, and then I realized how far she had come. That discrepancy seemed to justify everything, if everything needed justification. "It might be heavy," she said. "Certain people work out heavy relationships. That's the way they do it. Other people have to accept that. But if it works, it isn't horrible."

"No. I guess it isn't horrible."

"We know what we're doing. We're adults. We're consenting adults. It might not work for everybody, but for us it's a fine thing."

"As long as the two of you are happy."

Her mood had passed. She asked me if I wanted some dinner. I could tell by the intensity of her question that it would be a breach of friendship to refuse. I didn't. She cooked up some kind of meat patty. We offered some to sister Nathan. She said very gruffly that she didn't eat meat, and went on reading. I didn't ask her what was in it, but it tasted quite good, and I told her so. As I left she threw her arms around my neck and told me how happy she was now, and how good it was to have a friend like me. Her kiss was like a little moist peck on my cheek. I didn't need to worry about her any more.

I don't intend to think about those people ever again at all. Friendships come and friendships go. People grow out of each other. I don't feel responsible for what happened. When I think about it hardly anything at all seemed to have happened. It was natural. Two people followed their propensities into their own kind of happiness. This is the seventies. You've got to get some happiness while you can. They were better at working it out than most of my friends, but as far as I was personally concerned they were into something I couldn't relate to. Friendship, like everything else, is not forever.

When I got back to my place Gloria was burning incense in the dark and strumming her koto. She came over and sat down on my lap. She was like a feather. The only light was the glowing tip of the joss stick fanned by the air conditioner.

"Am I hurting you?" she asked.

"No. Not at all." I wasn't thinking.

"I thought I might be too heavy for you," she said, surprising me with a kiss on the eye.

"Well," I said. "If you'd just shift your weight a little, so I don't get numb."

That made her very happy.

ONE ON ONE

ONE ON ONE

six essays

on TAKING THE MATTER INTO YOUR OWN HANDS

this period of time seems to be closing : it was our time : I haven't prepared to move but I will leave anyway : I can hear the dredges working in the harbor : I am exactly behind them praising you with a mouthful of sand : how have we lived all our time among strangers and never opened the harbor before never got together before : you are right I'm alone : I now have something on my mind like wind I can feel under my wings : I build with feathers around my place : is it too late to ask if you can live in a house that moves in the wind : I am moving away to prevent the tyranny of song : this is speculation : rhythm is its enemy : I'll tie your freedom back from your eyes in this snood of words : you are under arrest : you are free to leave only by the entrance you found : yes you come in through an entrance though you imagine on the way that possibilities are endless : so it should not surprise you in retrospect the fact that you find me here

on THE PLAUSIBILITY OF FRIENDSHIP AMONG THE SEXES

once I have planted myself I cannot be moved : except by your gentle persistence : in that medium I am flexible but not much : because of me you need to maintain your strength : there could be something for both of us in a continuation of these meetings though there has been no real progress : I tasted the bread you baked : you listened to my latest report : that's as far as we go in this phase : now something else has to begin : come here again and put your mouth on my cock : yes : you are the boss : you are in the movies : please undress and wear that garter belt : squeeze your legs together : spread them apart : bend over : sweet puffy relaxed kiss kiss : do you like Japanese food : how much time did you spend in Corsica : go away if you have to sneeze : you aren't serious : now come back here and straddle my face : such a warm golden shower : I hate it : but these are the principles of our continuity : that I let you do things to me that I would never insist you let me do to you : you say you don't like it but you keep making these appointments : next time you will arrive by boat : I am thinking of mining the harbor

on PERPETUITY

it would be futile to continue this just for the sake of moving
you : I remain neutral : I prefer to tell you this
nothing : these lines are the essence of rumors : you know
too much already : you have already been moved too
often : I do not prefer to assert something at a moment when
you are indecisive : make your move : how many decisions
have already been made for you : make your move : I choose
to remain where I am outside the process inside this tent not
asserting neutrality but representing that capacity with the ease
of these words : if tomorrow changes my position it cannot
erase this track : neither you nor I will be here long enough to
witness all the testimony : this is no movement in the void
contrived to urge you beyond your boundaries : there is no
need to keep this going : nothing has been invested in the per-
petuation of this line : perhaps you will imagine as I once did
that you of all people were employed to keep it going : good
luck : I have no ambition now to influence you : doing this
isn't different from stopping at some point : that is why you
suddenly realize that you are still in motion though I was
finished long ago

on PAID VACATIONS

perhaps it is enervating to go on in this way but I have always
assumed since I need to do it that there is something I have to tell
you : so far that's not appeared to be true but you are still here
nonetheless : this serves as my reason to keep going : I wont
argue with you or myself or anyone else : move along that's
my motto : not much of a slogan but it keeps the crowd
shuffling past the exhibit so everybody gets to see some of it :
at this moment not much seems to be on display : growl : cackle : 'it's probably the wrong time of day
none of this seems to be moving' : 'darling I told you we'd
waste our time coming in the first place' : 'shhh he can hear
you' : can't hurt my feelings I never guaranteed you'd get a
thrill : if these words are stimulating you'll have to find out for
yourself : my legs ache : why would a person who values his
time want to come this far in my direction : ho hum : if any
of this ever gets moving again it's not my fault but the afternoon's and its policy of getting later : this has to be better than
a visit to some museum : you don't have to exhaust yourself
with admiration : if there is no benefit from reading this at
least you know it moves slowly enough so you can get off at any
point : at this point : you may even be relieved that these
words aren't chains binding you to some notions : if there are
any thoughts in this they are yours : take them away with
you : the advantage of reading here is this : when these
words stop you keep going

on SWIMMING WITHOUT GETTING WET

perhaps the meaning of these words will strike you : I apologize : those few who still remember the language may puzzle them out and accept them into their studies as an exhibit : I will observe their efforts but remain silent : I am silent now in such a way that you will come to understand : in the future they wont know us by our silence as we know ourselves but only by this palimpsest : so I continue to put these words down not to lead them astray but to give them something as I have been given something : notes about ourselves which have done me no good but serve at least to fill the imaginary volumes I carry on this portage : therefore I can't accept your busy refutation of what I have just said : your argument is perfect but your earnestness distracting : agree with me in essence because in essence you have no choice : my own feelings about the substance of this is unimportant because in summation these words are what I do : you have managed to go on saying nothing trivial : stop : if this seems much later to be some variation punch and judy show that's okay : at least we will seem to have spent this time together : goodby : I turn my back on these words now : I walk away from them now : they are left untold now : from the outset there was nothing said

on YOU AND ME BEFORE THE MILLENNIUM

there is nothing I can get from you though you can feel the
sapping at which I have become so proficient : whatever you
brought here you will take back with you though perhaps you
will notice that it now has some weight : that is the price you
have to pay for observing me as I act on myself : remember
you too are doing all this to yourself : you tried to kiss me and
you missed : I am over here holding out this mushroom for
you to eat : was it good : have a glass of Spanish wine : do
you feel it : now you are poisoned you will start to choke your
face will turn purple except your nose will blanch stomach
cramps set in and then you faint away : you will recover in
sixteen hours approximately : as you get better you will notice
I am still here taking care of you : I am eating a dish of the
same mushrooms I gave to you with a glass of Spanish wine : I
am immune to those principles which poisoned you : you mis-
trust my care and leave before you are fully recovered : at
home you imagine a relapse and study your condition in
bed : you surmise that something in you has been permanently
damaged by what you call the trick I played with
mushrooms : when you come to see me again it is to confront
me with the facts : our meeting is quite friendly and the facts
seem ridiculous once conveyed : nevertheless you have understood that the whole basis of our relationship has been irrevoca-
bly altered

MONGOLIAN WHISKEY

MONGOLIAN WHISKEY

A stuffed owl spun slowly in the breeze above the cash register when the man opened the door to let in his dog. Stanley crumbled the husk of a beer nut between his thumb and middle finger. "Big dog," he said, a little drunk, a little lonely. "You bet your ass," said the dog. He sniffed around the floor, got to the bar, scratched himself on Stanley's thigh. He had a rich, shiny coat, part black, part brown, and a white mask for his face. Some Newfoundland, and some Doberman in him, Stanley thought. He held a couple of beer nuts out in the palm of his hand, and the dog took them with his big mouth, hardly touching the hand.

"That's my dog," said the man who had let him in.

"That's my man," said the dog.

"Nice animal. What's his name?"

"We call him Tonto."

"My name is Tonto," the dog said.

"My wife picked the name. She's good at names."

"She's great in bed, too," said Tonto.

"It must be embarrasing to have a dog this smart," said Stanley, petting him some more. The dog left him to lie down at his master's feet. A cockroach stepped out from under the brass rail. "I'm from the endangered species defense committee," the roach yelled. Stanley crunched it with his boot. In the back room, under a rosy light, two couples were shooting pool. "Hey. You'll never get it in the hole that way," said a husky female voice. Stanley listened for more, but only mumbles and giggles followed.

"They don't let dogs into the bars in St. Louis," Stanley told the bartender.

"You try to keep this one out, you lose your door," said the bartender. Tonto let out a throaty woof. "There used to be a glass panel on the bottom of that door." Stanley looked at it, then at the dog. He could see it come crashing through the glass, its tail wagging.

"That must have been one exciting night at this bar."

"I wasn't here," said the bartender. Stanley was lonely a lot, travelling from one of these small empty cities to another, but he was still too sensitive not to feel slighted when the bartender turned to concentrate on the t-v, and Notre Dame basketball. "Yeah," said Stanley to himself. "It's all bullshit." He was starting to feel like one of those lonely travelling men he and his friends used to observe when he was in school, whose ranks he had promised himself he'd never join, lonesome, rootless Americans in the lists, making a little living serving Mammon Rockefeller et. al. "That's all over," he said to himself, thinking of his promise, thinking of the sixties when he'd been much younger, when his friends were together.

"Hey," the man with the dog said in his ear. "You think those are Jimmy Carter's nuts you fed to my dog?"

"Who?" said Stanley.

"Forget it. It's only funny once."

"Oh. President Carter. Sure."

"Didn't you vote for Mr. Peanut?"

"I don't vote."

The man grinned a little too broadly at him. He wasn't gay, but he seemed a little too friendly, a little weird. "I was in Chicago for the '68 convention," Stanley said. "Before that I marched in Washington, all that sixties political shit. I think Mayor Daley shook politics out of me. He's the only person I know with the first name of Mayor. I still don't know his first name, may he burn forever. Now I'm making a living like everyone else. Once I marched about twenty feet behind Martin Luther King."

The man put a hand on Stanley's shoulder. "We'll forgive you for that one. Let me buy you a drink." He ordered himself a glass of wine and another scotch and soda for Stanley.

"Are you from St. Louis?"

"I've been there," said Stanley.

"Where are you from?"

"I travel a lot. I used to live on a commune in New York State."

"We'll forgive that one too. General amnesty."

"It started good, but we broke up. We were each into something different. No one wanted to clean the outhouse. Things got too sloppy. Now I've been on the road for about a year and a half. I sell this educational equipment. Plug in a ghetto kid, pull out a genius. Could be a good job; I mean, the money would be great; but schools are too broke to buy much any more." Stanley suddenly felt like he was talking too much. He did that everywhere he stopped, at the slightest simulation of a friendly conversation. A few drinks and he was spilling more information about himself than he wanted to, more than anyone could want to hear. Anonymous mouths to anonymous ears. Talk.

"You're not far from Chicago here," said the man. "But Daley's dead there now, and give them a few years and they're going to eat each other alive, like a bunch of rats."

"Rats don't eat each other alive," said Tonto, in his sleep.

"It must have been great here," said Stanley. "When Tonto came through the plate glass window."

"I wasn't here at the time. Tina was. Tonto is my dog, but he's much more protective when he's with her. She's my wife. A good-looking woman."

"A real piece of ass," said Tonto, without lifting his sloppy jowls from the floor.

The man grinned and stared at Stanley for a long moment, as if he wanted the idea of a good-looking woman to really sink in. "Listen. My name's Charlie." Charlie was dressed neat and casual, in double-knit pants, his pale green shirt open at the collar, a pair of clean blue Adidas track shoes on his feet.

"Stanley," Stanley said, shaking hands.

The two couples came out of the back room and dropped some coins in the juke-box, goosing each other as they made selections.

"You don't think those people knew each other when they came in here?" Charlie said. "No way. They picked each other up. This is the only really loose place in South Bend. Nobody pays any attention."

Stanley watched the seduction game at the jukebox and felt vaguely jealous. In the blue and yellow lights from the Wurlitzer they looked like actors on a stage. If he'd gotten here a little earlier he might have been able to audition, who knows?

"I'll be right back," Charlie got off his stool, and Tonto got up to follow him for a few steps. "Going potty, Tonto." The dog lay down near Stanley.

"If I were you I'd ignore that dog," said the bartender.

"Tonto's a beautiful dog," said Stanley.

The bartender slammed the cash register drawer and one of the lines holding the stuffed owl snapped, so the bird swooped down and dangled by one wing. Stanley watched it wave back and forth. Its feathers were moth-eaten and tattered. The bartender took a slap at it.

"I'll tell you something," said Stanley. "If you want that owl to come back to life. I mean to really look good. If you want those feathers to shine again, what you do is take a pan, and fill it with salt, and heat it on the stove." The bartender wiped some glasses and looked at Stanley with minimum interest. Stanley was part of his job. "Then you take the feathers, the whole bird in this case, and hold it above the pan. Don't put it right down in the pan, but in the air above the hot salt. Feathers love that. They shine right up."

"Sounds good to me," said the owl.

"That's nice, thanks," said the bartender. "But to tell you the truth, this bird is just a pain in the ass."

"I'm giving you professional advice. My mother was a taxidermist. It's a trick of the trade."

"And my advice to you," said the bartender, as he yanked the bird off the ceiling, "is to lay off that dog."

"Nevermore," said the owl.

Tonto opened one eye. "You keep out of this, barkeep."

"Tonto is my friend," said Stanley, petting him.

"Yeah," said Tonto.

"A word to the wise . . ." said the bartender, as he carried the owl to the back room. Stanley watched the couples dance near the jukebox. They boogied just a little, then got real close, stood in one place, and practically did it right there to the accompaniment of Natalie Cole. Stanley felt like he was missing out. He often felt that way. Even when he was with a woman he felt that way.

"You must have an interesting mother," said Charlie, back in his seat. "I never heard of a lady taxidermist."

"I made that up," said Stanley. "But my mother drove a cab for a while, after my father died. The thing about salt and feathers is true, though."

Charlie grinned at him in a strange manner, tapping a picture he had placed on the bar. Stanley looked at it, then looked away. "That's my wife. That's Tina. Here." The man put the snapshot of the woman into Stanley's hand. Stanley looked from the picture to the couples grinding on the dance floor. There was no escape. The woman in the picture was naked. She was a beautiful naked woman, a face like Liv Ullman, with finer features, her hair dark blonde, puffed up in a kind of afro, skin the color of certain onions, pale-nippled plump small breasts, tiny waist, encouraging hips. Charlie was grinning.

"Isn't she a beauty?"

Stanley looked at him. "This is your wife?"

"Lemme see it," said Tonto, stretching to get up.

Stanley put the picture back on the bar, face down. Charlie turned the picture over. "Don't be embarrassed. She doesn't care. She's not ashamed of her body."

"Thanks for showing me her picture."

"That's okay."

Stanley watched the couples putting on their coats. They were ready to leave. They were going to someone's motel, or someone's apartment. All four of them had scored. Tomorrow he would be trying to sell a closed circuit video system, with a battery of foreign language tapes, to the staff of the South Bend superintendent of schools, if South Bend was where he was. Tomorrow was Thursday. Yes. Thursday was South Bend.

"How would you like to meet her?"

"What?"

"Don't be stupid. Say 'yes'," said Tonto.

"How would you like to meet my wife?"

"What do you mean, 'meet'?"

"Okay. I'll explain. I love my Tina very much. I'd do anything for her. And I know who she likes. I mean, we've worked things out pretty well. We have a relationship, which is more than a lot of couples can say."

"Amen to that," said Tonto.

"So occasionally I bring someone home for her. She's beautiful. She's a fine woman. She enjoys an occasional stranger. Why shouldn't she get her satisfaction?" Tonto was pacing back and forth along the bar. "We go home in a minute, Tonto."

"No sweat. Take your time," said the dog.

Charlie took one of Stanley's hands in both his. "All I want you to do is come home with me and make love to my wife. To tell you the truth, I like to watch." It was hard for Stanley to believe that this was a real situation. Something seemed to be missing. It was like a story he was being told by someone at a bar, bragging about his exploits, making it up. Was he really going to be that 'occasional stranger'? He couldn't believe that he himself was actually fielding this modern proposition, right in the midst of the blandness of his daily life, at this time of night, when he had planned only for a few drinks to relax himself, and then to bed. The big dog paced from the jukebox to the door. Was he actually present? Was this Charlie talking to him?

"She likes someone young. Someone who had radical politics

like herself in the sixties. Believe me, we're liberal. You are her kind of people. Look, if you think there's anything wrong with all this, just refuse; but I want you to know it's okay."

Stanley looked at this man, scanned the wife's picture with a beam of mild ethics, tried to picture himself crawling into bed alone in his motel room. Not a chance. He let out a long breath. He didn't realize he'd been holding his breath. "Okay."

"Why are you frowning?" asked Charlie. "It's not so heavy. You'll love it. Tina will charm the pants off you."

Stanley looked at the bartender. The bartender was watching the game.

Once he and the husband and the dog stepped out of the bar into the frigid air Stanley felt an incredible rush. Naturally this was the right thing to do, and right in the perverse heart of Middle America, in bland McDonald's white bread underarm deodorant America, in South Bend that in his rundown was characterized as the most average American city, and right next to Chicago where the cops had maced him and his friends in '68. He'd do it. He'd fucking do it on the grave of Mayor Pig Daley. He'd mace them with his own gisum, all the pigs that had come down on him and his friends through the sixties. He'd bring the weight of his thing down on them. He looked at the picture of Charlie's wife in his hand, and he felt very great.

They took Charlie's car, a giant Mercedes, a Janis Joplin dream, the first that Stanley had ever sat in, the seats beyond any idea of comfortable, just the right amount soft, yet firm enough to let you feel solid, supported but really there. And the car was warm inside. And the radio and tape deck — an incomparable Blaupunkt.

"You like this?" Charlie asked. "This is Tina's car. I have an Alfa, but you can't start the thing when it gets this cold. I used to drive my Avanti, just to keep the old Studebaker idea alive in South Bend. But I don't like it. You feel like you're steering a boat. I keep it in the garage."

Tonto stood on the back seat, big head leaning over into the front, breath steaming the windshield.

How much money did this guy have? And it was there with-out pretense, obviously old money. This couldn't be just some guy who had made it rich. Stanley didn't mind wealth at all when it was carried this easily. It made him feel comfortable, in fact. What a peculiar bar, that one; and to make a friendship like this one there. "Do you go to that bar a lot?" he asked.

"I like it there. You meet people not necessarily run of the mill South Bend. It's not uptight like most of the other places in this town."

By the time they got to the circular drive leading to Charlie's big old house Stanley had nearly forgotten his reason for com-ing along. Charlie's company was friendly, and he was reassur-ing in his easy generous way. Stanley had been right in begin-ning to suspect that as he got older prosperity could dim for him some of the questions that once had burned.

It was an old house, but the interior was totally remodelled, turned into something he wouldn't have expected could exist in South Bend. All the walls and most of the ceiling had been removed leaving a large open space with areas separated by beautiful screens, some of them contemporary in design, some oriental. The walls were white, all white, making Stanley feel he had walked into a cloud. Above the mantel was a colorful painting shaped of arcs and half circles, by Frank Stella, who had been among those Stanley had condemned in the late six-ties, after studying art himself for a while, for being decadent bourgeois, but whose work he admitted to himself now looked very beautiful in the indirect lighting of this dreamy space, and it made him feel that he might have done better to pursue a purer interest in art at the time, for this painting looked almost like a Navaho rug, and who could accuse the Navaho, who are so poor, of being bourgeois for creating their own abstract beauty in the desert?

"There she is," said Charlie. Stanley caught just a glimpse of the wife, who appeared for a moment on the balcony above the room. She appeared again, coming down the curved stairway in a pale yellow diaphanous toga. Stanley suddenly remembered why he was there, and felt his spine soften, like a snake gone limp, and he felt a slight nausea as he watched this beautiful woman make the most of descending the stairs.

"What do you think of her?"

"I'd like to sit down." Stanley found a chair, and sinking into it felt as if the whole room was pitching, as if a storm was going on forever. He wouldn't tell anyone, but he was scared.

"I'll bet you're from New York," were her first words to him.

"You're close," he said.

"I'm really glad you're here," she said.

Once again Stanley didn't realize he had been holding his breath. "So am I," exploded from his mouth.

"What did I tell you?" said Charlie.

"You're from Boston?"

"New Jersey," said Stanley, "West Englewood." The woman made him feel a little more comfortable. She was very natural about it all. She sat in the chair opposite, with her hands folded in her lap, leaned forward for the interview in a slightly awkward position. He hardly noticed that he could see her body through the sheer yellow veils. Tonto lay down at her feet and watched him. She covered the dog's eyes with her small hands.

"I can understand if you feel funny about this, but it's okay. Charlie never makes a mistake. I know I like you. But I'll call a cab if you've got second thoughts. You can leave now."

"No," Stanley sighed. "It's alright. I've decided to stay."

"You make it sound like a tough decision," she said coyly, and tucked her legs up under her butt on the chair, and leaned back so the transparent cloth pressed against her nipples. Stanley turned to Charlie, who was watching them with great interest. "Something like this doesn't often happen to me; I mean I don't even expect it to happen." He turned back to Tina. "Do other men who come here seem different? Are they more relaxed?"

Charlie moved to the back of the chair and started to massage Stanley's shoulders. "Don't worry so much. You're exactly what we want." He smacked Stanley's cheek. "He was in the peace movement. He marched with what's his name?"

"Martin Luther King," said Stanley.

"Yeah him," said Charlie. He pinched Stanley's arms. "He's very tender." There was a new note, an almost sinister undertone in Charlie's voice, that made him believe there was more going on here than he understood yet; but that was their problem, and he wasn't going to be around long enough to dope out their problems. He just came along to get in and out, so to speak. He smiled at this joke himself. So what? It was easy enough to be comfortable in this place. He leaned back into the cushions. "What happens now, folks?"

"Now, I'll leave you two alone for a while," said Charlie. "So you can get friendly." He started upstairs. "Come on, Tonto." The dog followed him. Tina got up and walked back and forth in front of Stanley. Her bare feet sank to the ankles in the pile of the rug.

"I get a little nervous about this too," she said. Stanley took off his shoes and stood up. "I'm even a little shy," she said. "Maybe that's why I like to do this. It makes me feel innocent, like a virgin again. It's like we're newlyweds." Her smile was so sweet. Charlie was right. She could charm the pants right off him. "And don't mind Charlie," she said. "He's bound to get into his own trips. He'll even play jealous. He loves that." She put her arm in his and led him to the stereo. "You know where I met him?"

"I have no idea," said Stanley.

She flipped through the records lying on the counter. "I met him at the trial." She held up the Stevie Wonder KEY OF LIFE album for his approval. He shrugged.

"At the trial of the Chicago Seven?"

Stevie Wonder started to sing. "Yeah. The Hoffman Follies. I was in Iowa City, and went to Chicago just to see if I could watch it. No way I could get a seat, until Charlie picked me up and took me in with him. He said it was the best entertainment in the country." They started dancing nicely.

"He must be very rich."

"Don't ask about it."

"Where does his money come from?"

"Didn't come from anywhere. He always had his money."

"Do you love him?"

Tina pressed closer to him. "Yes. I do." Her body stiffened when she said that, making him want to soften her in his arms. She seemed very vulnerable, open to intimacy with him. She stroked his face and smiled. "Say. How would you like a taste of Mongolian Whiskey?"

"Why not," he said. "I've never had it."

She poured some burnished golden booze out of a smoky grey bottle. "It looks like Yak piss," he said.

"Charlie's private stock," she smiled.

He sipped it. There was a smoky taste, like blood sausage, and a slight bouquet of semen, but it was smooth. "It goes down nice," he said. "Once you defeat the smell."

"Contradiction and struggle are universal and absolute," she said, and took a sip too.

He drank some more. It was quite potent, especially on top of the scotch he had been drinking. "That was from Chairman Mao, right? The quotations?"

"I knew them by heart," she said and walked around in front of him with her whiskey glass, as if modelling clothes. She was the most beautiful woman with whom he had ever had the prospect of making love. And where was he? In South Bend. And where was that? In Indiana. He had promised himself once never to stop in Indiana. Gas up in Ohio, drive through to Illinois. But now he was happy to be here. He watched her body move in the transparencies of yellow toga and felt a rich mixture of anarchy and alcohol rise to his brain.

"Well," he said. "I'm ready. How do we do this thing? Lead me to the place. I think I want to do it."

"We should always use our brains," she said, and sat down next to him, "and think everything over very carefully." She kissed him. "A common saying goes, 'knit your brows and you will hit upon a stratagem'." Almost as if he hadn't willed it himself Stanley's hand floated over to caress her breast. The breast was warm.

"It is not enough to set tasks," Tina touched his elbow, and they stood up. "We must also solve the problem of the methods for carrying them out. If your task is to cross a river, we cannot cross it without a bridge or a boat."

"Let's find the bed," said Stanley.

"Right thinking."

"Chairman Mao," he said. "Look at me now."

"Investigation may be likened to the long months of pregnancy, and solving a problem to the day of birth. I used to really like that one," she said, kissing him again. "Appealed to what used to be my predilection for motherhood, forgotten, thank god, before it was satisfied." She led him around the room, sitting on various couches and chairs, taking him on a tour of the place. He found her exotic and wonderful, unpredictable. He tried to embrace her, just to still the light quaking of desire in his own body. She stepped back. "All erroneous ideas, all poisonous weeds, all ghosts and monsters must be subject to criticism . . ."

"Now you're being coy, Ms. Chairman."

"How do you like my place?" she asked.

"You mean the room?" He looked around. "It's as beautiful as you are, and very tasteful, and still full of surprises."

"I designed it myself, you know. I'm a designer. The furniture is all my design."

"Far out," said Stanley. "Have you designed other places? You've got lots of talent."

"Guard against arrogance," she said. "Even those who have made no mistakes and have achieved very great success in their work should not be arrogant. All work done for the masses must start from their needs and not from the desire of any individual, no matter how well intentioned."

"I'll go along with that," said Stanley. At one time Chairman Mao had seemed to him correct in his analysis of every situation. Here he was being led around now through a dream maze of unresolvable contradiction. Surrender, something told him; watch your ass, said something else. "Why don't we fuck?" said Stanley.

Tina pulled back a screen behind which a large circular bed loomed, a pool of fur and satin. "Where do correct ideas come from? Do they drop from the skies? No. Are they innate in the minds? No. They come from social practice and from it alone." She pulled back the coverlet and started to unbutton Stanley's clothes. He finished undressing himself as she undid her toga and lay down on the satin sheets. This was experience ala Chairman Hefner. "Pleasure seeking," she said. "There are also quite a few people whose individualism finds expression in pleasure seeking. They always hope that their unit will march into big cities."

"Hush," said Stanley. "Make love, not war."

"There are not a few who are irresponsible in their work, preferring the light to the heavy, shoving the heavy loads onto others and choosing the easy ones for themselves."

He swallowed her voice with his mouth and covered her body with his own. She moved like a wave. The little angels of erection peeked for a moment from behind their curtains, and then withdrew again. "Too much Chairman Mao," he whispered in her ear, "dulls the militancy of lust."

"Make trouble, fail, make trouble again, fail again . . . till their doom; that is the logic of the imperialists and all reactionaries the world over . . ."

Charlie had entered without a sound and sat watching from a nearby love seat. Stanley saw him. Tonto rested on the love seat beside him, his eyes covered with a black hood, like a hunting falcon or an executioner. This was a weird experience, Stanley thought; more than he'd bargained for. Only Tina was reassuring, as she seemed intent on his and her own pleasure. She stroked him with a gentle pressure, wiping his fears away. "Fight, fail, fight again, fail again, fight again . . . till their victory; that is the logic of the people." Erection was accomplished with all its apparent authority. She closed her hand around it.

"Political power grows out of the barrel of a gun," she said.

"I was waiting for that one to pop up," Stanley grinned, and positioned himself over her.

She whispered in his ear, "Thousands upon thousands of martyrs have heroically laid down their lives for the people; let us hold their banner high and march ahead along the path crimson with blood!"

"Today is a good day to die," Stanley yipped softly, like Crazy Horse, in her ear, and he moved on her.

Charlie took off Tonto's hood. "Tonto," he said.

"With pleasure, boss," said the dog.

Stanley heard Tonto say that, and then he heard the big dog roar, but before he could move he felt the weight on the bed, and the mouth, and the rip between his legs. "Yum," said Tonto, and a tongue of molten steel seared into Stanley's being and then the teeth at his throat. "Omigod. I'm dead," he said and never found out if anyone had heard him.

Tina raised up on her knees and elbows and Tonto licked her back. "Please get it off the bed, Charlie," she said.

Charlie pulled the twitching body to the floor. "It's a lot cheaper than canned food."

"Long live chairman miaoooo," Tina barked, as Tonto wedged into her, most of her head and neck in his big bloody soft mouth.

Stanley hovered above the scene. So that was the whole shot. Life was over for him. A surprise, he admitted, but more relaxing than he ever would have anticipated. He felt really maneuverable as he watched with some curiosity while Charlie cut up what had been his flesh and packed it into freezer bags. "I wonder if the bartender knows their racket?" Stanley asked himself. Charlie had almost everything cleaned up. Tonto and Tina were stuck back to back, both of them looking a little embarrassed and impatient. It was too boring to watch this. This was the stuff of dull old life. Effortlessly Stanley rose through the ceiling. That was a new experience, real fun, something worth dying for. Shuck the body and rise. It was morning.

South Bend was soaking in a muddy light. Someone else would have to sell them the educational video contraptions and electronic sandwiches. Glad to be free of that. There were some banks opening, and some small skyscrapers filling. The fast food dispensaries tuned their machines. There were the golden arches of McDonalds, and there was the golden dome of Notre Dame. He flew a holding pattern above it, waiting for further instructions. The students and faculty moved below in an unrelenting milieu of college life, of dull chauvinism and school spirit, of genteel subliminal brain damage. Suddenly he noticed a man in a black cassock fading back from the formation of students moving to class. He had a football in his hand and he was looking at Stanley. "Oh no," thought Stanley. He didn't stand a chance. The man in black pumped once, twice, and released the ball just before he got sacked. Stanley had never caught a football in his life. He had bad hands. Now he regretted it, after his death. Too late. If he had it to live over again he would certainly have tried harder to catch a football. But this pearly blue pass, coming his way, not a chance. It went right through his hands. He turned, and watched it go on rising, and he couldn't help but follow it through the cool, crackling veils of fire that billowed up around him out of nowhere. What a feeling. He was a tender being of light that kept on rising, kept on rising until the ball hit the uprights supporting the glimmering gates. He dived on the ball and recovered it. When he looked up he saw three winged dogs standing around him, a Golden Retriever, a Rotweiler, and a St. Bernard.

"You got any I.D.?" the Rotweiler said.

Stanley had left his wallet in his pants back with Tonto, Tina, and Charlie. All his credit cards were in there.

"You can't go in without proof of grace," said the St. Bernard.

Stanley stood up and held the football awkwardly in one hand. He threw it as hard as he could. "Fetch," he commanded. "Go fetch the ball, rover." It worked. These were well-trained dogs. They took off after the ball, and he sneaked through the pearly gates, thanking Notre Dame in his heart of hearts. It was great in there, like entering a car wash. Sudsy clouds of beige fluff, and pink and yellow engulfed him, wind whirling like brushes inside it, and all the smells of frankincense and myrrh, of sandalwood and roses washed across him like a wave of detergent. He felt something like a sharp slap on his butt, and busted through to the porcelain blue clarity of heaven. The place was full of dogs. They buzzed him on their gossamer wings, wagging their tails, making passes at him with their spirit tongues. Every breed was barking there, and all the mongrels too. As far as he could see he was the only human being in heaven. He'd never read anything about this. Whole cadres of drowned puppies went yipping by in a state of grace. Mongrels and purebred expensive Lhasa Apsos consorted in squadrons with Borzois and mutts. Heaven was dogs. They all barked and yapped at him in their heavenly voices. What a revelation.

Stanley turned back to where he imagined the earth to be. "Hey, you guys," he shouted. "There's nothing but dogs in heaven." He looked around again. It was the truth. He shouted louder. "There's dogs up here. Just dogs. There's all kinds of dogs in heaven." He knew it was useless to warn them. Americans don't listen to the dead. Even if they could hear they wouldn't hear. Down there it was youth culture, up here it was dogs. He'd like to tell them, but he guessed they'd have to find out for themselves. Stanley looked around at the doggy paradise. Nothing for him. He looked above into the wide empty realm of stufflessness. That's where he was going. He did a lonely little frog kick and kept on moving.

TWO SEASIDE YARNS

TWO SEASIDE YARNS

I

GREED

The other day as I walked my dog down the beach and watched him sniff the breeze I happened to cut my foot on a piece of rusty iron that was sticking out of the pebbles. Sandpipers scooted, terns flew back and forth, stabbing at the water. I was bleeding profusely, but I thought that before I treated myself I would perform an act of good citizenship and rid the beach of this hazard. I strained my back a trifle pulling at the old piece of iron, but there was no way to free it. I got down on my hands and knees and scraped back the pebbles to see what held the iron fast. It turned out to be an old barrel ring, attached to a very old barrel, that had probably been buried on this beach years before they built the breakwater, and only now was the barrel being uncovered. On its lid one word was burned: AFRIQUE. I rushed back to my campsite to get a tool that would crack open the barrel. My two kids and my wife came back to satisfy their curiosities as well. They were quick to call divvies on whatever sunken treasure we found. With great difficulty we freed the barrel from the stones and turned it upright. It weighed a ton. I pried at its lid with a tire iron. It wouldn't budge until suddenly it flew off, and the tire iron slipped from my hands and crushed my wife's nose. We were all astonished at what we found within, all of us except my three-year-old daughter. We hadn't

noticed the tide was rising. We lost her. A big wave pulled her
off her feet, and a riptide dragged her out to sea. There was
nothing we could do. I still haven't got over it. The barrel was
full of tiny, delicately carved ivory elephants. Some of them
were still alive, and when they saw us they climbed over the
backs of the dead ones and marched around the rim of the barrel
like their big counterparts in the circus. Naturally my dog went
crazy when he saw the creatures. He treated them like rats,
crushing their delicate, hollow ivory skulls in his big jaws. The
only way I could stop him was to club him with the tire iron. He
was finished, and it's a shame. In every other way he was a nice
dog. Dead or alive those elephants were worth a mint. The three
of us looked at each other. We didn't dare say it, but we felt like
profiteers. And we were rich ones. We closed the barrel and
slowly pushed it up the bank to our Chevy. Each of those
elephants weighed only a few ounces, but I wouldn't want to
estimate the weight of a whole barrelful. One time the barrel
rolled back on my son. His legs and pelvis were crushed, but we
got it up the bank, and into the Chevy, and deciding that discre-
tion was the better part of valor we left in a hurry, not bothering
to even pick up our tent and camping gear. We headed home
with our find. When we were stopped at the light a colored man
approached and started to engage us in conversation. I didn't
catch everything he said, but something to the effect of, "Hey,
jive turkey, you peckerwood toejam motherfucker," was the
gist of it. "If you want to get anywhere in this life," I suggested
to him, "You'll have to improve your English. Take this, my
good man." I gave him one of the elephants my pooch had
crushed. "Hey, motherfuck," he said, as our Chevy pulled
away. "I'm gonna motherfuck you motherfuckin' motherfuck-
ers." I had forgotten completely about my wounded foot. It
wasn't until after we got the living elephants into the birdcages
at home that I tried to treat it. By then it was too late. I lost the
leg, and decided on a peg-leg instead of a prosthesis, because it
seemed appropriate. The elephants sold out — four hundred
apiece for the dead ones, eleven hundred for those still moving.
Now we've got lots of things. Traded the Chevy for a Caddy.

Bought this yacht. My wife is happy. She wears a veil, but lifts it when she shines up my peg. We have more fun now, even as a family. I had a wheelchair made for my son out of the very barrel-staves our fortune came in. We have three little elephants left. One whistles like a canary. The other two are lovers. What I enjoy now is things like when I put a rollerskate on my good foot and stick my peg into one of the holes on the deck of our yacht. Then my son comes by in his wheelchair and pushes me around. I spin like a top. It's better than working. Or my wife attaches some muslin wings from my arms to my belt and I turn like radar in the wind. I did that for them at Gibraltar and they loved it. We love it too.

II

NEED

That's the sea. Finally. Now you have to do without a beach chair and an umbrella. No cabana for you, darling. After all you bought that little white elephant from the black man and spent too much money. Sure he was nice and polite and poor, but I still say he was too damned expensive. And what use is a little white elephant? Anyway, there's our sea. We can't go any further in this direction. If we turn around it's back to the mountains, and what can you do there besides jump on the rocks? You go back there if that's what you need to do; I'm going to stay right here and watch that there old raven peckin' at the wrack. Look at his buddy trying to coax him away, swooping up and down, but my old raven figures these big waves are bound to wash in something. That's the way I feel about it. Stand by the waves long enough and you'll get some good stuff. Wait a second. What's that riding in on that big wave? There goes the raven. Whatever it is, he doesn't want it. I think it's

coming in for us, honey. Let's climb down this bank and get it.
Wait a minute. Look at here. Just what we need. This is a great
big penis, and riding on that penis is a gorgeous mermaid. Put
away your elephant, honey. You take the penis and I've got the
mermaid. Now I bet you're glad we came to the ocean. See you
later. Hello, miss. Pucker up. Ouch. You've got scratchy scales.
Keep your tail to yourself, and let's just talk. Must get lonesome
riding around all day on a penis. Come on, you could stab a man
to death with those fins. What I was saying was that a penis
doesn't make a man, and a man doesn't make a penis either.
Sure I could get fond of your tits, but I need the rest of the
anatomy to get roused up. If you've got a sister at home who
carries the bottom half bring her along next time. Honey, you
about done with that penis? Where'd you go? Good God. Your
penis has jaws, miss, and it just ate my wife. That's not fair. I'm
going to miss her. Once a man has a wife, he needs a wife. You
get out of here and take your penis before anything else happens. Damned mermaid, ruins a vacation. There she goes on the
penis that swallowed my wife. But I'm not one to cry over spilt
milk. Mermaids aren't all they're cracked up to be, and neither
are giant penises. I still believe in the seashore more than the
mountains, but at this point nothing could be satisfying, and
now I'm alone. Hey, what's this coming in now? It looks like a
bed. It is. It's a waterbed. Too late. Thanks a lot. Now we've lost
each other and now I've got this waterbed. Hello raven, watcha
cravin'? What the hell. Have an elephant. No? Okay, see you
later. Fly away. Can anyone believe what has happened to me
on my vacation? I feel empty. All that's left for me to do is sing
my song:

> Hello.
> My name is Steve Katz.
> Have pity on me. A giant
> Penis ate my wife, and now
> I'm left alone, with a tiny
> Ivory elephant, and a waterbed
> On the beach.

TWO ESSAYS

TWO ESSAYS

on COLLABORATION

It is always gratifying to do something, get deeply involved in it, work it out, and then suddenly relax and forget about it. Go away, go to sleep, go to the movies, take a long vacation. When you return you find that someone else, someone you love, has picked it up where you left off and has changed it; someone who was aware from the outset of an area of potential in what you were doing that you had totally ignored. She works on it, and something rare and fine is the result, something you wouldn't have imagined or accomplished yourself. You can't resent it because it is someone you love who has made the effort and effected the transformation. So what if she has distorted what had been your intention, made it a little too dainty, whereas you had intended to convey some kind of rough energy. You two are partners after all. She loves you so much that she can't resist helping, and you clearly left it around where she wouldn't be able to avoid tinkering with it. You both stand there looking at this thing with which neither of you is quite satisfied, and perfunctorily praise each other's participation in the effort. Neither of you likes it, really. It's actually quite ugly. You are both secretly disgusted with it. If you didn't love each other so much you would probably throw it away. It will probably disappear anyway, through neglect; besides, someone has forgotten completely to cook the mackerel you enjoyed catching this morning.

They have been lying in the sun and now are beginning to stink. "If you'd worked on the potatoes instead of that we'd have a mackerel casserole." "You didn't tell anyone you were going fishing." "They were lying there all day in front of your nose." "Just because they were lying there doesn't make me like fish better." "They're starting to stink. The least you can do is get rid of them. I caught them." "I won't touch them. They stink." "Yeah. They stink." You both sit down and say no more, refusing to admit discomfort from the swarming flies. Flies were keeling over with delight. That was why when we found you both we had at first this awful revulsion, and then this amazed interest. Your pictures are in the paper this morning. You look ambivalent, but content, both of you. The caption reads: NEW FLY SPECIES BREEDS ON HUMAN COUPLE.

on LEADERSHIP

I'm not a thinker, I'm a doer. I haven't done it yet but I imagine I'll get it done some day. When I do, I'll show it to you. Meanwhile, let's play cards. Pinochle. Someone says I cheat at cards, but someone is wrong. I just get good hands, golden hands. Hands that make me wish I were a gambler. I'm not a gambler, I'm a man of God. When the time comes I'll pass on the word. You'll be the first to know. It's your deal. That's a poker deck. Poker will corrupt a man. Pinochle's a pastime. That's the word. I don't want to play now. Let's take a walk. Speed it up, but not too fast. Moderation is the word. Those are my neighbors' lawn mowers. Those are my neighbor's dogs. It is perfect here except for one thing. Anything. Nothing's perfect. This is the edge of town and out there are the woods. The dogs are barking at something in the woods. I feel at home in those woods so follow me. Evergreens. Hardwoods. Underbrush. Moss. Mushrooms. You are in danger. Yes this is a gun in my hand. I was afraid

you'd be too bored to walk in the woods and I want you to keep
going. Keep going. Sit down. Deal the cards. That's the Queen
of Hearts. When did you sleep with my wife? Why not? It's in
the cards. I'm not a jealous man but I value my wife. You didn't
know I was married. I'm not. Why did you corrupt my little
daughter? Shut up. When did you last repair a pot-hole in the
road? I'm not anti-establishment but I believe everything could
stand some improvement. Suck in your gut. Eyes straight ahead.
I brought you here to have this talk. You'd better talk. Shut up.
I'm not a man of words, I'm a doer of deeds. This is what I do.
This gun is made of soap. Wash your mouth with it before you
speak to me. The stream down there is polluted by the factory
up there. That's why the dogs are barking. That's why I brought
you here. To bark. To start an investigation. Everyone is coming
into the woods. I invited them here because you need some
advice. Settle down. You have been chosen as our leader. I am
your leader. There will be witnesses. We are going to have a
meeting and you are the Russian premier. These are affairs of
state. Why did you try to escape to the woods? You have something we need and we won't let you leave these woods until you
give it up. This place has been declared unfit for human habita-
tion. Do you want to live here? I'm not an architect but I have a
sense of order. If you were God is this how you would have
made it up? I am God. Just come towards me. You're the man
who fucked the wife of God. Take one step at a time, very
slowly, two steps at a time. How do you feel now? Is this the
cure? You're a little tired, but that's natural. I'm not a doctor, I
start from scratch. I don't play the game myself, but I'm a hell of
a coach. Now you get out there and kick some ass.

SMOOTH

SMOOTH

for Janet Rifkin

It won't upset you to understand that I am a salve, though some have mistakenly called me an ointment. I am satisfied that no one yet has called me a pomade, or an application, or a preparation (ugh).

And this is how it went. Completely went.

"I don't have time to be in love, Steve-O." That was bullshit, because I knew Strawberry already loved my bro. I believe he loved her as well; but I loved her differently. My bro is black. These are the seventies. That's what happens, so don't ask. It's not boring. This is America. Boredom is not one of the blessings of our time.

How do I feel about it? Am I some grease? Am I the soft soap?

Wednesday night was usually ours, Strawberry's and mine, and I always looked forward to it, because she knew how to use me in a way that filled me up. Does that seem impossible? Impossibility is the fuel of relationships between the sexes (among the sexes? throughout the sexes?). I don't know how to say it any more. Language at this time is such a dense slush of approximations. But please don't get me wrong; there is no similarity between my nature and the quality of slush.

I did half a day of my own work which is, for want of a better expression, 'free lance' work, and spent the rest of the day preparing for Wednesday night. At one time it had been my lovely Dawn, who liked to meet me in a wide-mouthed jar, so getting ready for her had been a question of filling it to the brim.

And my beautiful, goofy Arizona would take me in a paper cup, a rusty ladel, a wooden shoe, anything out of which she could dip me with her long fingers. But for Strawberry, and I'm not complaining, I had to fit myself into a tube, not a plastic tube, (she hates plastic), but a flexible, lead-alloy tube that she rolled up from the bottom as she used me.

Have you ever tried to fit everything, your spirit, your heart and mind, your whole sensuality, and all of that swollen and weighted with love, into such a tube? After vowing not to get a wrinkle, not even a dent, in the tube? It takes me at least half a day, and then I'm exhausted. I was so exhausted on Wednesday, April 10, 1974, that while I was waiting for Strawberry to get there I fell asleep on my own sofa. If I could only tell you what I dreamed.

At 8:15 a knock on my door. It wasn't Strawberry. She had sent my bro. Here he was. A change was coming.

"What's happening, Steve-O?"

"It's what you see, bro."

That was the first time we had ever talked in hip, ghetto, jive, or whatever jargon. A new formality had entered our relationship.

He slipped me under his coat and we left. It was snowing lightly, the streets covered with a slippery quarter inch, the kind of weather that makes most noses run, but causes me to stiffen up. He slid most of the way to his apartment on East 7th while I stayed soft inside his coat. His was a large basement apartment, 3 & 1/2 rooms, 2 & 3/4 of which were taken up by his bomb. His bomb. It left space in the apartment only for a hot plate and a single bed. Strawberry sat on the bed, nibbling some dry figs. He opened his coat and I think she was glad to see me. I was glad to see her, though a little put out by this change in our Wednesdays. 'Our Wednesdays'. What a romantic idea, makes me nostalgic, like the title of an old movie.

Have you ever done what I was doing? Or imagined yourself doing it? To be there in the love nest with the woman you love and her lover? I would never have expected to have such objectivity, to find their way so fascinating. It was even reassuring to observe the relaxed banality of their relationship. So little said it seemed like hostility. So few caresses. So much between them misunderstood. Their lack of tenderness was thrilling. No closer than two riders feeling each other up in the subway rush hour. I wondered if I could ever understand what was going on between them.

He kept looking at her as if she was in the way, and he could punish her at any moment. She seemed afraid to violate his macho and confront him with the trip he was running on her. What vibes were these? Was it racial? I'll never know. At one point, just to get away from her, he walked into the bomb itself. I wished I wasn't there. I was glad I was there.

"You're pissed," she peered into the recesses of the bomb.

"No, baby. I just got something to do in here."

"You could've done it before I got here. You act as if only your time has value."

No one acted as if I was there.

"Shit," from the depths of my Bro's bomb.

He was more relaxed when he came out. Exhausted, I'd better say. It's always touch and go inside a bomb. Suddenly they stretched out on the bed and quietly embraced, just holding each other, just as I had done myself with Strawberry on Wednesday nights previous to this one. Curious that I didn't feel jealous, crowded there against my own Wednesday night Strawberry. I didn't know if they were ever going to remember that I was present.

Do you prefer the clear, the translucent, or the opaque?

Then there was a knock on the door. Bro sat up. "O mama I forgot." Three young men entered. Wicked was first, wearing his green beret, his skin smooth and pale brown, his small fist raised in greeting. When he saw the white girl, Strawberry, on the bed, his face seemed instantly to register several decisions he had made and would act on without conscience. His eyes actually narrowed. Strawberry pulled herself into a corner of the bed against the wall. Ronnie Small was next, an enormous man, so black his skin seemed to consume light. For some reason they called him 'Bug'. His fist was as big as my Bro's face. "Who's that? Your hostage?" His grin was friendly. He was one of those big men who in order to put people at ease in the presence of his own massiveness feels obliged to be always jolly. Silk posted himself outside for a moment, watching the street. His real name was James Thomson, but they called him Silk. He raised his fist and entered. He did know how to glide into a room. My Bro included, these four men were a conspiracy. They met on Wednesday nights.

Silk pointed at Strawberry, "Get it out of here."

"She's cool," said my Bro.

"She goes," said Silk.

No one had noticed me. If she needed help I could have employed the element of surprise, which in these situations is the only element I know.

My Bro pulled her off the bed. "Sorry, Berry." He shoved her into his bomb and locked the door behind her. At least she had the presence of mind to grab me on the way in and we were locked up there together, two of us, Wednesday night, in a bomb. I really liked it. She moved me as deep into the weapon as we could go. She didn't want to hear the slightest mumble of the revolutionaries. We sat there in the near total darkness. Her own sighs so close to me warmed me up.

"I'm so confused, Steve-O. You'd never treat me this way."

"You must like it. If you put up with it."

"It was always easier with you."

I didn't know why she was saying this now. She should have known that I still had some feelings. She squeezed a little of me into the palm of her hand and smeared me across her forehead. She knew from experience that I left no greasy film. Perhaps that's what she meant by 'easier'. No inert ingredients. I was beginning to see something now in the dim yellow light. My Bro had included everything you'd expect in his bomb. The World Trade Center was in there. Chase Manhattan with money ripening. Naval bases at San Diego. The Verrazano Narrows Bridge was there, I don't know why. Everything. C.I.A. heroin complicity. Whale-slaughter. You know what was in there better than I do. This conspiracy was small only in its number of conspirators. They were conspiring against the conspiracy of conspirators.

"Strawberry," I said. "How can you live with this bomb? Do you understand what it's about?"

"This is more complicated for me, Steve-O."

"Don't you talk to him about this?"

"He never let me into his bomb before."

"Explain to him that violence is reactionary, Strawberry. It plays right into the hands of power-freaks and fascists. A revolution has to be regenerative." I spoke with such passion that I couldn't believe myself. I usually don't have that kind of idea — a so-called 'political opinion'. That was the day I discovered the counter-irritant principle in my nature.

Strawberry was crying. "I hate love, Steve-O. It's so degrading."

"Why are you telling me this?"

"I want to do my own work. I want you to help me."

I knew she didn't really mean it, but she looked at me. She really looked at me so I almost began to flow, as I once did on our own private Wednesdays. She squeezed me out a little bit to rub some on her lips, and behind her ears, and down the long slide of her neck.

"Do you think they'll look for us down here, Strawberry?"

"O Tom, I'm so scared."

"Maybe I'll blow out the candle so we don't waste it."

We played Tom Sawyer and were feeling real creamy and giggly when my Bro opened the door.

The conspirators were gone. My Bro stood in the doorway shifting the box of shotgun shells he had been given from one hand to the other. As soon as she saw him Strawberry rushed his way at ten million light-years an hour. Time surrounded me like a cage.

No, not sticky, not gummy, not tacky.

They undressed. He held on to those shotgun shells. She went after his flesh with her tongue, nibbling his breasts, plucking his ribs, sounding his belly with her lips, down on his thighs, mouthing his small, dark cock. He placed one hand on the back of her head and hefted the box of ammunition with the other. He closed his eyes. Perhaps he experienced pleasure. I don't know. I was there, and I was not there.

She stepped away, her back to me, and looked at his body. There was no erection on him. She took his shotgun shells and placed them on the floor next to the bed. Then she looked back at me in the grey apartment light. Suddenly I understood that I was to be an intimate in their arrangement. She began to apply me to his body. She spread me over the dark amber rise of his collarbones, and rubbed me into the curls on his chest, and down his long brown belly so I pooled up in his navel. His muscles shone like a weightlifter's with me. She anointed with me his pelvis and thighs, smoothed me between his buttocks. His cock lifted like a cannon.

"We're going to get that stuff all over my clean sheets and blankets," he said.

"Don't worry," said Strawberry. "I'll wash them for you."

To be referred to as 'that stuff' didn't bother me, but Strawberry's uncharacteristic offer of domestic service to my Bro made me feel awful. She had never washed a dish in my house. That was my one jealous moment.

Then he took me by the gob into the palm of his hand and fondled me onto her breasts. Over her ribs, the soft bell of her hips, down the insides of her thighs. She was open and big and wet. I was their slipperiness. We were together.

O pinguid unctuous lubricious blup blup shlosh ooonnppaaahh.

I have to admit to you that I enjoyed it.

"Thanks for last Wednesday. You showed a lot of character." Strawberry on the telephone. So official.

"Character?"

"Well then, forbearance. Tolerance."

"Strawberry, it wasn't any of that. I enjoyed it."

"O good. I was afraid we might have lost our special thing."

"We have lost our Wednesdays."

"Well, yeah. But that's what I'm calling about. Next Wednesday."

"Three of us again?"

"That's how it adds up."

How do you say yes? How do you say no?

My Bro visited me one day in the middle of my work. He looked around my apartment with obvious distaste.

"How do you go on living in this place?"

"What's wrong with it?" .

He shrugged, shook his head. "I didn't come here to apologize, or explain anything."

"No apologies expected."

"I did cut you out of your Wednesdays and I'll explain it. It was bad for my head. I'm just telling you."

I had nothing to say. I had no reason to complain. Everyone has a life to work out. It's a crowded planet. I don't think he was saying what he wanted to get said. Maybe he didn't know what it was. "I mean if she stays with me you know she's white and she's going to have to work really hard and be subjected to discipline."

"I got that."

"All you could do is fuck up her head for us, you know what I mean. She's got to see things clearly."

What was it? Did it make any difference? These were words. Some human sounds. Loud and soft. It would never get said. It would never get said.

"Besides," he said. "You're just weird. I never knew anyone could be like you. You're a mess. You live in a mess. You're too weird for the revolutionary consciousness." I took that as a compliment. There was no way that he could understand at this point in history that I have chosen the softer way.

I'm a salve. I'm not a pomade. Not an ointment. Not a cream.
None of those things. Used properly, I am a salve.

On the day my brother's bomb went off New York was frozen. The edge of a low-pressure system from the Gulf of Mexico
was bumping against a high-pressure system from the Great
Lakes squeezing a stationary front that lingered just South of
Asbury Park. Cold winds were sucked into the city under the
turbulence in the upper atmosphere. New York bodies
shrugged under weighty overcoats. Fingers froze in the glove.
Noses poked out of red woolen face masks. Breath beads of ice
on a million moustaches. A city of spoons that banged on old
radiators.

That I mentioned the bomb in the first place probably made
you suspect that it would go off, because that's the way a story is
told, especially this one where there seems to be a conspiracy
present. I won't apologize for this cataclysm. It always happens.
The bomb went off. I was there. Strawberry was there. My Bro
was there. Bug, Wicked and Silk were there. There was a meeting and Strawberry was allowed to listen in, and I was ignored,
as usual, being just the contents of my tube.

"I can't think about Wounded Knee. Don't tell me about it."

"It's all one revolution."

"Yeah. But we got enough to do right here."

Almost as if on cue, with the word 'here', the bomb went off.

I suppose it was a catastrophe, but from my point of view
what was most interesting was the change of state that I experienced. I'll try to explain, because I am sure none of you can
report such an experience. Being of my own consistency the
experience wasn't the violence of the explosion for me, as it was
for my Bro, Strawberry and the others in the conspiracy. They
were immediately dismantled by the violence and dispersed,
whereas I was swiftly spread thin. I am not so devastated as they
by a change of state. Your credulity will probably be tested by
what I tell you next, but I'm going to say it, if only to help you
once and for all to grasp the distinction between a salve and all

that other stuff I have mentioned, like some lotions you might know about.

I was able to focus on each detail of the explosion and slow the whole process down. I observed that it would take virtual lifetimes to unfold if only I could maintain my focus. I started by watching the ignition, which can be observed in itself as a process of explosion infinitely attenuated as time is slowed. I saw the explosion expand as a geometric series of individual ignitions of particles, each one, then two, then four, burning more brightly than the ones preceding, as the burning of each fueled the 'ardor' of the next. They separated as they flashed, the speed of separation in inverse proportion to my power of attention. (Unfortunately such an experience happens only once. Given another shot at it I could be a much more acute observer.) The space around the burning particles contracted and expanded slowly in such a way that I felt penetrated by something like a wind, as if all of space was a kind of bellows. Little wavelets of wind, each wavelet containing some heat from the source, accumulated into this breeze I experienced, a breeze that, if I hadn't been in such close attendance on what was happening, could have hit me with the force of a tornado. Light began to change color. A slowly paling green. Magenta. Violet, a dismal brown, orange. Then colors for which I have no name. Sound began. At first a tiny bell that I didn't believe I'd really heard, until another and another rang, and I was surrounded by bells, a world of cathedrals gonging around me, and I was suddenly part of this space opening of distant twinkling particles speeding away. That was the last I apprehended of it. My attention must have strayed just long enough for this change of state. I can't tell you what caused my mind to wander like that. I blew it. I always do. I've always had a lazy mind, but that's me.

All my molecules blew loose. What a feeling. Now they bound around with the molecules of Strawberry, and of my Bro, and his conspiracy, and whoever else was affected by the conspiracy's explosion. I love it. I love them all. I love everything. I have learned from this condition that love is the gassy state. I love you. We are all cozy and equal in these motions. You have divine orbits, and as for me, I am still a salve, and come to think of it that quality is unique to my nature. It wouldn't be true of a pomade or an ointment. Old problems float away. Strawberry and me, Strawberry and my Bro, Strawberry and you. Everyone and Strawberry.

THREE ESSAYS

THREE ESSAYS

on TAKING THE CURE

come in : this is my tent : you carry the sickness : please be seated
: the spider's web stretches between this tent and the sun : pay
no attention to it : you passed this way before but I have never
seen you like this before so sad so sloppy so tired : pardon me
while I push my cock through this jellyfish : ahhhhh : if I am too
personal too tender too slick don't let me bore you : I live here
without the common elephant : do you wear those clothes to
intimidate your friends : I don't want to go anywhere with you :
this place is the place : brains don't impress me you didn't have
to carry yours all the way down the path : you told me a story
about a man who had everything he needed in the world except
one thing : he needed oxygen : out of luck poor devil : but you
have come to the oxygen tent and here is your oxygen : you will
need it before you leave : now sit on the floor of this tent : I am
selling you this kit you will find valuable any time you want to
make some snow : ahhhhh : do you find my language exalted
abusive ablative : if this were February you wouldn't have made
it down here : I never asked you to come but now you need some
advice take the first left take the first right keep on rising : I am
not an astrologer : this is not the age of reason : listen to that
sound it's the noise of the sea : sound it's the noise of the sea : the
noise of the sea : it tells a complicated story about the car you
left by the road : why did you come here : you have a flat tire :

your muffler is punctured : you are crazy beyond help : pardon
me while I stick my finger into this flight of birds : these sur-
roundings are in perpetual motion : so be it : and so you have
recovered from the sickness : goodby : this is not small wisdom
this is not big wisdom : these are empty statements full of syn-
thetics : this is nothing doing : what are you doing here : I'm
trying to close up : I spoke all this in order to keep your attention
: now forget it all you can leave that's the cure : the spider has
trapped our cloud as it covered the sun : I think your payment
will be ecstasy : I think your success will be absolute : as you
leave you will make note of the moon

on HIDDEN BLESSINGS

excuse me I was watching the stars : I haven't had time yet to
read your application or your manuscript : I agree it's past noon
but I watch them on my own schedule : who are you : why did
you bring your manuscript here to my tent : I'm in no position to
recommend you for anything : I can't comment on the quality of
your soul : let me look into your eyes : you have a scummy soul :
    your soul pisses in its own bed : get it up : don't let your soul
loose without a chaperone : now here comes my soul : look out
soul : let's watch them : sh : they are dancing : no : your soul is
fucking my soul : no : my soul cooks soul food for your soul :
    no : our souls have heated up this tent and now we're in this
hot-air balloon : we are drifting over Miami : the people of
Miami Beach are waving at us from their wheelchairs : there's
Cape Kennedy stay away from it : too late here comes one of
those mamalickin F 111's : our souls have left us here to die :
you steer the tent I'll hit that plane with this axe : hold 'er steady
: oof : got it : now ease her down : you're doing great : come to
think of it our souls did okay too : we make a good team : now I
know you well enough to help you out : here's my advice : settle

down somewhere in the midwest but don't get married : sell farm machinery or work for the liquor commission : raise a fatherless child : write two books based on your childhood in Buffalo New York : call them FROZEN STEEL and FUDDLER ON THE ROOT : publish the first one with Alfred Knopf : this is the beginning of your second book : you can have it free : I don't need it : your career can have my career : I have spoken : now I'm going to close my eyes again : don't mention anything I have said or anything that has happened here : don't tell anyone else where I am

on THE DIFFERENCE BETWEEN THE 60'S AND THE 70'S

somewhere else something wonderful has captured the imagination of the young : I intend to go there and insist on their freedom : I do not expect to use force or display my wicked arsenal of banality : I will free them by persuasion and talent : I will use all the money at my disposal : come with me but bring your own poems : perhaps we will find when we get there that the problem has already been solved : in that case I shall have to wrap you in your poems and ship you home : I don't relish that responsibility : on second thought I would prefer that you stay here and keep my place in order : here is lumber : build whatever you please over the hole after I emerge : there is grain & lentils & beans & rice & lentils : eat them I'm leaving : I wont be back : this is tuesday : this is wednesday : this is saturday evening : I have arrived in Pennsylvania after an impossible trek : the people are inhospitable and the city is crowded : I have nowhere to go : I have to rent a cheap bed in a flophouse : O I have no money : I am going to sleep on the street : I'm glad I brought this bundle : Good Night

DEATH
OF THE BAND

DEATH
OF THE BAND

for Philip Glass

He felt two small hits as he listened to the music from the bandshell, as if he had been struck by some pebbles; in fact, if he hadn't glanced at his shoulder and noticed the blood that was seeping through his t-shirt he wouldn't have paid any attention. Now he had two wounds.

One listener behind him tapped on the back of a bench with his umbrella, one slept. A scantily dressed girl turned away when he caught her eye. There was no one else on the benches. Then he saw the composer, cradled in the lowest branch of a large maple, aiming his gun. He gestured for Arnold to move aside. Arnold moved, embarrassed to be in the line of fire. A parabola of dusty light suddenly filled part of the hollow in back of the musicians, then clouds covered the sun again and the composer commenced firing rapidly into the bandshell.

The gun had a silencer, but the audience could hear the shells ricocheting inside the music. The affect was thrilling Americana. Then the musicians began to fall. It was in their contracts that each of them keep playing until he is hit in the head, which happened on the count of seven for some, three for others. Once all the players had fallen the performance was over. It was then that Arnold, who had got out of the way, began to feel guilty for the death of the band.

Peter leaned back against the tree trunk and cradled the weapon in his lap. This was the first piece he had written following strictly his ideas of irreversible subtraction. The performance had been exquisite, as good as his music could be played.

The instrumentation, the live performance, the composer as performer: everything was coming together. A nice surprise was the role the audience took on its own, like a tragic chorus. This was a dramatic dimension he couldn't have predicted. Peter himself had worn the maple tree as if it were a mask. It had become more than drama. It was a ritual, and he was the shaman. How interesting. No way to predict it. It was worth all the psychic hernias that one got dealing with the art world in the seventies, just to make these few discoveries about one's own music. He sat in the maple tree mask and enjoyed the little applause and fondled the instrument he had played so well. It was just a 22. Everything had become the music, even Rumi, his sound man, backing a van to the stage to get the equipment. They had to get out fast. The bandshell was to be used again that evening for a free performance of the Pro Musica Antiqua.

Arnold passed through the zoo to the south end of the park pressing one of his wounds. The hit on the shoulder had just scored the flesh, but the one that had pierced his back was still bleeding. He could touch the little slug lodged between his ribs where the flesh had stopped it. If he took it to the hospital that would involve the police, and endless explanations, and put his favorite young composer through a lot of paralyzing legal rigamarole. And he might have to explain about the band. He didn't know how to deal yet with his responsibility in that regard. He had moved out of the way. Would the band still be alive if he had stayed put? How to answer that one? He propped himself against the park wall and slowly slid to the west side. Maybe now he had become just part of the music, turned loose in the city. Now he didn't regret skipping work, because he had got to witness a rare performance of the music he loved, a premiere performance, that had moved him greatly, that had become a part of him in these two wounds that complicated his response, a slug lodged in his ribs like a dangerous bit of information. But he hadn't figured it out yet, just how he felt about the death of the band.

The Detective touched the bodies with the toe of his wing-tip

shoe. Eight of them, all longhairs, each hit in the head by a small
caliber bullet. It was neat, the work of a skilled marksman, so
clean, very little blood spilled. He didn't want to flatter any-
body, but this was good work. He knew right then that this one
would go unsolved. He'd do the paper work, but no arrests
here. It would blow his statistics. His rate of convictions was
already too high. He was becoming a better detective, but he
didn't want them to expect too much of him. They'd start to
push him. They'd want to make him a Lieutenant. He couldn't
take that. Out of respect for professionalism he'd let this one go
unsolved. The hitters he ran into these days all had long hair, so
either way this was some kind of low-life snuffed. He pulled out
a pad to write down the number 8, and noticed that an enormous crowd had gathered. "The turkeys are gathering," he
muttered, his voice amplified by the bandshell. The audience
applauded. "Bullshit." He turned his back on them. He didn't
like this kind of caper, where he ended up on a bandstand. He
hated the public eye. He liked the old-fashioned idea, so hard to
come by in the seventies, of a murder in a boudoir.

They came from the rowboats, from Bethesda fountain, from
the merry-go-round, from the zoo, and they kept coming, climb-
ing down over the rocks, busting through the bushes. This was
amusing. This was human interest. This was the biggest crowd
the bandshell had seen in years. "Everywhere is punks," said
The Detective, scanning the audience. They applauded and
cheered and whistled. Ice Cream wagons, hot dogs. Pretzels.
Balloons six feet long. Sparkling yo-yos. The networks arrived.
Camera buffs by the dozens joined the police photographer,
calling out f-stops and shutter speeds.

The Detective knew it was time to leave it with his men in
blue. He scrutinized the bodies draped over the music stands
one last time. One thing he had learned for sure from the
spiritual practices he pursued to help ease his mind in this tough
line of work was that none of these deaths meant anything at all.
That was something of which he was convinced. Not even a
drop in the cosmic bucket. He couldn't worry about individuals

any more. They were a lot of skin stuffed with punks as far as he understood it. That was why he was becoming a better detective.

Arnold still had the key to Betsy's apartment, though they rarely saw each other any more. He let himself in. Betsy was a pisces and a liberal, full of cloying displays of generosity that he found tiresome; but at this point the prospect of Betsy wiping his brow and loving him a little was the only good possibility he had. Her apartment was sloppy as usual, dishes piled in the sink, soiled clothes on top of everything. He put his finger on the lump between his ribs. The bleeding had almost stopped and the pain was down to a dull ache. He scrubbed out one of her pots and boiled up her French paring knives. He felt remarkably clear, and unafraid of what had to be done. He wished there was someone with a video port-a-pack to record his excellent moves. He ripped an old sheet into strips and boiled them, found Hydrogen Peroxide in the medicine cabinet, laid the strips of bandage over the bathtub, and sat down on the toilet seat with a paring knife. Betsy's knives always had a surgical edge. He thrust out his rib-cage, keeping a finger on the lump of lead, and then touched the point of the blade to his flesh, punctured, opened himself between the ribs. The slug squirted out over the bathmat as if it had been waiting to complete its trajectory. He felt as if he had suddenly shed twenty-five pounds. The stinging of the peroxide was wonderful. He rose with it as if from dream to dream. He hadn't needed a hospital. He didn't have to tell anyone about the death of the band. He could hang on to the wonderful feeling Peter Glucks' concert had given him.

He went to Betsy's bedroom, messed up as usual, vaginal cream open on the night table, applicator fallen into yesterday's underwear on the floor. He sat on the bed and thought about telling her everything, because Betsy would understand, because at one time the deepest bond between them was a mutual love for the new American music. He leaned back on the pillow as the pain struck him, and he passed out.

"You people are as prejudiced about us as we are with you. You better believe it. You don't have to be so condescending with me," the Detective told the girl who had joined him at a table in the museum cafeteria. Betsy blushed. He was probably right. She had no business asking if he was a cop. She touched his sleeve. "I'm sorry. Sometimes I don't think before I speak." He sure looked like a cop, but sort of attractive.

"I don't want to implicate you as a hippy, but you ought to be aware that hippies have their own prejudices." Since he had started occasionally snacking at these museums he had been getting a lot more ass, and that made him a better detective.

"I'm sure that's true," said Betsy. "The hardest thing to see sometimes is yourself." She detected a surprising sensitivity in this man, and he was alive, tuned in, not like those people she usually spent time with, bored, stoned or frightened. This man was refreshing.

"People find out I'm a detective and they right away have some ideas like 'Excitement,' they think. 'French Connection.' Like I found eight musicians, or something, shot through the head in the bandshell this morning and I bet you instantly think, 'Heavy. Adventure.' "

"Eight musicians?"

"I don't know musicians from toll collectors. Maybe they were joggers. But they were all shot through the head, and what that means for me is another long boring routine. A routine. A good detective has to appreciate a routine. I am in love with boredom. Here." He takes Betsy's hand and presses it to the gun under his jacket. "What do you think that means? Anything?"

"I think it's horrible to have to live with a gun all the time."

"It's a routine. It's like your tampax. I use it once a month. Most of my work is paper work. I file reports."

"There were really eight musicians killed in the park this afternoon?"

"It's a new American hobby. Mass murders. You're lucky it isn't California. Eight is a drop in the bucket there. What's your name?"

"I'm Hilda," said Betsy. She didn't think it would be cool to give a detective her real name. She liked the strong, thick hands on the table, the cleft jaw like two small boulders.

"You live around here, Hilda?"

"I live across the park."

"I don't like to beat around the bush, Hilda. I got a tight schedule. Let's go over there now. You know what I mean."

Betsy looked away, as if she needed a moment to decide, but her mind was already made up. It was a thrilling and slightly kinky idea. The Detective got up. "No offense meant. If you don't want it I'll understand. But let me pay for your Tab." She let him do it, the first time in years she had let a man pay her bill. She slipped her arm in his as they left. No one had any idea who she was. This was the strangest thing she had done since she was a teenager. "I don't know if those guys were musicians or not. They could have been parkies . . . interns . . . foreigners . . . She pressed close to his body. They left the museum through a display of South Sea artifacts.

"In most places they won't let you hunt with a crossbow," said the salesman.

"I'm not going to hunt," said Peter Glucks. The instrument was fiberglass, very fancy, fitted with a brass sight and trigger, and a small brass winch to draw the string back; but it wasn't what Peter had visualized.

"Where do you intend to use this weapon?"

"I'm not sure it's really what I want," said Peter. "Do you have anything made of wood, like polished cherry or birch?"

"I haven't seen one made out of wood for years. It's not practical. Where will you use this weapon?"

It was something more medieval that he had in mind, something carved and elegant. "It'll just be a small hall," he said. "No more than three hundred people." The piece was scored for viola da gamba, harpsichord, recorders and hunting horn, all of them amplified. It needed a special environment.

"I'm sorry," said the salesman. He took the crossbow away from Peter Glucks. He wasn't going to be the one who sold a deadly weapon to a madman. "I don't think we have what you want."

Peter didn't protest. This was the kind of resistance to his art he faced wherever he turned. He was used to it. Things would work out. When the time came to perform the piece he'd have his instrument. He would face more troublesome problems when he returned from his European tour. He had a recording session then, and that was infinitely more problematic with his new music than a 'live' performance. He was thinking about videotapes, recording the new work on videocassettes. That would make his new music a star. He left the Sporting Goods store. The crossbow idea wasn't so touchy. A more delicate problem was his piece for koto, piccolo, and blow-gun.

"Shit," said Rumi, when Peter got back to the van.

"What's wrong?"

"We got another damned ticket."

"Well," said the composer, philosophically. "I suppose we'd better pay this one."

Betsy gasped when she saw Arnold lying in the mess in her bed. He had grabbed the tube of contraceptive cream as he was passing out, and had squeezed it all over the sheets. "I'm not the neatest person," she told The Detective, who was snooping in every corner. She slapped Arnold's face. He was really out.

"I'm meticulous," said The Detective.

"Are you casing my joint, or something?"

The Detective stopped at the foot of the bed. "Is this the junkie you live with?"

"This is Arnold. He's a good friend."

"I deduced as much," said The Detective. "But does Arnold stay or do I go or what?"

Betsy lifted the bedsheet and saw the dry blood. "He's been hurt," she said.

"We've all been hurt," said The Detective.

"Get some cold water," she said, feeling Arnold's pulse. "I wonder what happened." The Detective shrugged and went for water.

"Your kitchen is for pigs," he said, returning with a bowl. She swabbed Arnold's forehead with a wet rag. "Look, Hilda honey, either he's out of here in ten minutes or I'm leaving."

"Come on. Have a heart. The man's hurt."

"Sweetheart, a little blood is no new thing from my point of view. He looks okay. He moves."

Arnold opened his eyes. "Betsy," he said, touching her face, leaving a smear of contraceptive cream on her cheek.

"What are you doing in my apartment, Arnold?"

"Dying," he smiled.

"Who shot you?" she glanced at The Detective.

"Not interested," he said. "I'm off duty. This isn't my precinct." He went back to the kitchen.

"Peter Glucks," Arnold told her.

"The composer?"

"It was part of the music, the way he ended the piece?"

"Shooting you was music?"

"It wasn't like that, like it was me he shot. I was between him and the band, and he was shooting the band. I don't know if I was part of the music or part of the audience. But I moved out of the line of fire and then he shot the band. He shot it in the head. It was wonderful."

"What did it sound like?"

"I mean it was horrible, but you felt that it was some important music, and I was involved in it. I mean I was morally involved. That is a real innovation. It was my choice to move or not . . ."

"He shot everyone in the band?"

"What's all this Liptons?" shouted the detective from the kitchen? "Haven't you got any good tea?"

"Who is that?" asked Arnold.

"He's a detective. I brought him here, we were going to ball, but I didn't expect you . . ."

"Don't tell him anything. Nothing. Don't say I'm here."

"He knows you're here. What can I say to him?"

"Say I was bit by a dog. Say I was in a fight. This music is very important to me, Betsy. It's turned me around. I can't explain it yet but my whole attitude to myself and music is different. I'm . . . I don't know."

"Arnold, this detective found eight musicians dead in the Central Park bandshell today."

"I know, Betsy, and I'm trying to understand if it was my fault."

"How is it your fault?"

"Betsy, I moved out of the way after Glucks hit me. The band might still be alive if I hadn't moved, I think. Maybe not. But I have to figure it out."

"O Arnold," said Betsy, wiping up the vaginal cream. "Only a Jewish person would worry about that. You had a Jewish mother."

"What difference does that make? I even took the bullet out by myself. Look." He exposed his wounds as Betsy headed for the kitchen.

"He's really been shot," she said to The Detective, who had finished looking in all her cupboards.

"I don't want to hear his story. All I know is you don't have a decent cookie in the place. And you buy this gummy peanut butter."

"He says he was shot at the concert in the bandshell. By the composer. By Peter Glucks." She enunciated very carefully, with great solemnity. "Doesn't that ring a bell?"

"Honey, everything rings a bell in this city. Nobody's to blame. Nothing's wrong. Everything's wrong. Everyone's to blame. Everything happens here and we don't need an explanation. It's all criminal activity. Nothing causes anything. Everything causes everything. That's the rules. Now why would a girl like you fill her breadbox with Wonder Bread? That's murder. That's suicide. You're just lucky I'm off duty."

Arnold stood in the door of the kitchen as straight as he could. He was white as a slice of bread. The wounds throbbed a little but he felt okay. "I . . . I think I'm going to leave. You guys want to use the bed, so go ahead. I'll go home. I feel pretty good.

I just want to talk to Betsy for a minute." He took Betsy's hand and led her out of the kitchen. "I'm sorry, Betsy," he whispered, "that I've driven you into bed with detectives." Betsy was touched. She and Arnold once had a very intense thing going. Tears dampened the corners of her eyes. "Relationships. Fuck them. I'll always love you somehow, Arnold," she said. "It's all so impossible," he said, and went out the door.

"Aren't you going to do something?" she asked The Detective as he stepped out of the kitchen.

"Just shut up. It's not your business." He came at her down the hallway. "Shut your woman's mouth." He twisted her arm and pushed her against the wall. He grabbed her head and dug his thumb in just under the jaw. No one had ever hurt her like this before. She could feel his fist in the small of her back. "Look, I know now your name is Betsy, not Hilda, but I'll let that go. You're lucky I'm not on duty. Just stay out of my business and stop trying to make this into a movie. Now do your little trick for me."

She believed she hated him, but there was nothing else she could do. Her hand grazed his cock as she turned. It wasn't even erect. That made him more dangerous. She knew she'd better do it with him now, even though Arnold had wasted all her birth control. At least she'd learned from this experiment that her prejudices about such men as The Detective had some foundation. She'd never make a move like this again, but for now it was too risky not to fuck. One consolation was that if it did happen to her, abortions now were cheap and easy.

After that day time passed at a certain pace for everyone: endless for Arnold who was going through the deepest changes; frantic for Betsy who cursed her luck when she missed two periods; for Peter Glucks time seemed not to pass at all; and The Detective put time aside and monotonously assembled evidence.

Arnold never left his room. Once he had consumed all the food in his cupboard he started a long fast. He had a sense of purpose; there was something he needed to do. That concert

had changed his life, a great compliment to the young composer. His two wounds became two scars, a permanent inspira-
tion to Arnold. He turned his friends away at the door. When
his office called he hung up. His longest phone conversation was
with Betsy, who for three quarters of an hour described her
abortion to him. "Is that all," he asked, as soon as she stopped
talking. He wanted to remain alone and silent. "Yes, but I . . ."
He hung up. After that Betsy changed the lock on her door. She
realized that for her Arnold was a lost cause. He was getting
thinner, contracting around his two ripening scars. They were
the fulcrum of his new understanding, a petroglyph incised in
his flesh. They held like amulets the special charms of his new
understanding, that the music was something outside the mas-
tery of an instrument, or knowledge of harmony and counter-
point. He was reaching for a new, ineffable reality where art and
experience coincide. He practiced the guitar every day. He
hadn't played for years because he hated to hear himself. He had
always been lousy, and a worse singer; but now it pleased him
even to sing. And so what? He'd get through it. He was still
terrible, and the hours of practice didn't help. So what? He
realized now that the art wasn't in the guitar or the ordering of
the sound or the invention; it was somewhere else, somewhere
he was grinding himself to go, somewhere he had first been
given a glimpse of when he witnessed, even participated in, the
death of the band.

  The Detective continued to piece it all together, just for the
exercise, for the art of it. It wasn't happening too slow, and it
wasn't happening too fast. His mixture of indifference and
devotion made him a better detective. Long hours got him home
late and he fell asleep with his service revolver on. When he
woke up his mind was full of thoughts. Were they true? Were
they false? He was being led to several inevitable conclusions.
Did they matter? He was glad to be alone. He took off the
revolver and the clothes and put on some pale gold pajamas. He
set a cushion on the floor in the center of his living room and lit a
joss stick. "Fuck the lotus position," he said and crossed his

legs. Almost as if he had flicked a switch he emptied his mind of thoughts, erasing a whole week's work. His lids floated down, his pupils floated up. Men and women. Good and evil. What the fuck? Hot and cold. Colors sifted through and stabilized as pure white light in his skull. It was all the same. He had a job to do. Work and play. Guilty and innocent. A clear pleasant bell began to tinkle in the void he was attending. It entered his position through the left ear.

His new music made Peter Gluck's life more complicated, and most of what he spent his time doing had nothing to do with making music. The hassle of booking concerts, setting up tours, arranging accomodations, all fell on him since he wasn't popular enough yet to afford a manager. His work was classified, unfortunately, as 'serious' music, and serious music didn't make bucks. So the chores were his, and he actually enjoyed it, even shopping for the peculiar instruments. Now he had a wonderful old crossbow, with quarrels made of ebony and brass. More complicated was that he had to continually rehearse new musicians. He never thought he would find players enough willing to perform his new music, considering the consequences; but that wasn't the case. Every week at least two or three would show up at his loft with a viola or a clarinet and ask to be in the band. They all knew what that meant, but they wanted to learn the music, and as one older player said, "It's safer than walking the streets in the city these days." And everyone played the music with enthusiasm and dedication. A whole new breed of exciting young musicians was finishing their careers playing his music. It was thrilling for Peter, and only his sure sense of priorities prevented him from turning it into a power trip. "No. No thank you," said a very talented flautist when Peter offered, as he always felt obliged to do, to buy the man dinner before his performance. "I'm fasting today, anyway."

He had finally found the bass clarinetist he needed to complete the band for his Chicago concert: two electric pianos, an amplified violin, a trumpet, a singer, and the bass clarinet. The voice was a new notion. It didn't totally work yet, but there was something very rich about it. The fall of a singer might make the performance a little too much like tragedy. That wouldn't work. It had to be a delicate balance. But it was only February 14, and he had till April to get it right. The singer was really good, and good looking. She had been a model once, and had studied voice for years, had specialized in lieder. And there was something about her that touched him personally, but he couldn't let himself get involved. He had too many plans. It would be unprofessional.

The singer answered the doorbell. Arnold was there, dressed in his fatigues. He hesitated a moment, squinting into the light, and then stepped inside. "Is this Peter Glucks?" His voice quavered slightly, as if too finely tuned. "Right," said someone sitting at the piano. Arnold set his instrument case on the floor. That he was moving very slowly made everyone pay attention to him. There was something new about Arnold's manner, something fine and ascetic, a pure glow. He could be someone you almost feared, but someone you also aspired to be.

"I want to audition for the band," said Arnold.

"That's weird," Peter said. "You're number eight today."

Arnold looked at the singer. "What's your instrument?"

The way he said it made her blush. "I sing with the band," she said.

"I love you," said Arnold. "I want you to help me."

"This thing is growing so fast it's scary," said Peter Glucks. He pointed at Arnold's instrument case. "If that's a guitar, man, I'm sorry. I've never really written a piece for guitar. There's the pop-country-folk stigma that keeps me away from it. I know that's just in my own head, but I haven't really dealt with it. But I really do appreciate that you came to see me." The composer laid his arm somewhat patronizingly on Arnold's shoulder. "I really have no use for guitar, but leave your address in case I write something."

Arnold slipped the composer's arm off his shoulder and stepped back. He unbuttoned his shirt and slowly opened it to reveal the two gleaming scars. "Do you recognize these?"

The band closed in for a look. Peter Glucks ran his finger down the scars. "O how strange," said the composer. "I almost forgot that piece. You were in the bandshell. You were heavier. Weird. There was something in that first piece that I still . . . wow."

"It's lovely," said the singer, kissing both scars.

"Thank you for coming by, man. I'd almost forgot how that piece worked." He ran the backs of his fingers up the piano keys. "The music never ends. Ideas just grow one out of the other." He tapped his forehead. "I can't believe how fantastic."

"Do you want to hear me play my instrument?"

"Of course, man. I'd really dig to. I might do a piece for guitar. Who knows. I'm open to anything. Go ahead."

In the fluorescent light everyone seemed made of enameled steel. Arnold unsnapped his case. "I don't sing very well," he said to the singer. "Can you come and sing with me?" She smiled and crossed the room to stand next to him. He lifted his instrument out of the case. As soon as she saw it the singer sang. Arnold stepped in front of her and put the butt of his instrument to his shoulder. The singer burst into her own rendition of East Side/West Side. Arnold opened fire. "All around the town," sang the singer. There wasn't time for the composer to even sit in on crossbow. The whole ensemble fell in every direction as they were lunging for their instruments. It wasn't the greatest performance, but it was Arnold's first, and he played as well as he could. The responsibility for the death of the band could now unequivocally be laid on him. He embraced the singer and they backed out the door. She was still singing and he lightly patted the beat on her arm. Something special had happened between them. They were a new duo, a direction of their own in the new music. The elation made them laugh when they hit the street and lost their voices to the traffic, thrilled with their discovery of each other; and they skipped away to Chinatown, singing and holding hands.

BUMPKIN

BUMPKIN

He piloted his thing over the peaks of intellection and landed in the valley of discernment and pitched a tent close to a current fed by freshets in the Spring. This was Autumn. He hated 'to fish' but he was hungry. Gazing upon the water he saw them at swim and thought, "No." Town seemed uninhabitable at this point, but he took the long trail to the supermarket, bought the frozen codfish, lugged it back to the campfire, and broiled it on a lattice of green willow. They couldn't annoy him by lifting their heads from the water to laugh. So what? He loved the codfish cooked just so, and his intentions were his redemption – to sort the imaginary, to codify the real. He figured there was always tomorrow to adjust; but sometimes tomorrow didn't come. Sometimes tomorrow was too late. Sometimes tomorrow was chainsaws and chokers and giant balloons to float the big timber back over the mountains where he never wanted to go again. He never wanted to think again. He wasn't lonely. The six people he knew to be himself had grown to forty-three. That was thirty-six (the square of six) plus four plus three or seven, his lucky number; so he felt safe as well: the safety in numbers. His craft had disappeared anyway and like an idiot he had forgot his sleeping bag. He shivered by his fire. Throughout a fine night for looking at the stars he stared into the flames. He stared into the fire.

MADE OF WAX

MADE OF WAX

On the day that Anthony discovered he was made of wax he received a telegram from the foundation informing him that his application for a grant had just about been approved and that the members of the committee were anxious to interview him at his earliest convenience. He made this discovery as he sat close to the fire in his tipi, reading the telegram a second time. His left hand wilted. He watched it change shape as if he understood what was going on, as if he knew he was dreaming. The telegram seemed even stranger. So much time had passed since he applied for the grant that he had forgotten about it; in fact, he doubted that he had ever formally applied for anything. He got great pleasure now from living in the woods. He would never consider packing things up and returning to the city just for an interview. He had things set up cozy — a big tipi in the wilderness, half a day's walk to town, mountain stream nearby. Eat grouse, blueberries, and plenty of chanterelles, his favorite mushroom. Best of all he had Holly, and they had a thing going. The melting hand was not problem. Wax was easy to work with. He was a craftsman.

"Hey, read this, will you?" He handed the telegram to Holly.

Holly put down the binoculars and took the telegram. She shook her head. "I bet you won't even go to see them. You're not a fellowship kind of person. You don't even care about it."

"I haven't made a decision yet," said Anthony.

"You'll never make a decision. You're too casual."

"I'm happy doing what I do right here, and I want to be with you, Holly. Besides, I don't think I even applied for a grant."

Holly leaned back on the mattress to look through the binoculars at the stars shining through the smokehole. "I know I'm not going to leave here, not till I see the skylab space station pass over my smokehole."

Anthony sat down next to her. "It'll never happen, Holly. The orbit is wrong. The smokehole faces the other way."

Holly rested the binoculars on her breast and said softly, "I paid my taxes last year. I'm an American citizen."

Anthony went to the fire again and squatted to reread the telegram. A grant? From a foundation? Not likely for him. His hot arm was bent back at the middle of the forearm now so the knuckles were fused to the elbow. It looked peculiar. Holly had gotten up to go outside. Anthony threw the telegram into the fire and followed her. The foundation's message burned crisply.

"Look at this," he said, then he saw that she was pulling the lacing pins out of the tipi. "What are you doing?"

"I'm going to turn the tipi around so the smokehole is facing the orbit of skylab. I want to see the manned space station pass over the smokehole. That's why I came here."

"Holly, that would face the smokehole into the wind, smack into it, and you wouldn't be able to see anything because the smoke would blow down into your eyes."

"I don't care."

"Besides, it's crazy to try to move all the poles around in the middle of the night."

Holly sat down and looked at the stars. Anthony sat down and looked at Holly. "Do you want to see something?" he asked.

"Yes. I want to see the skylab manned space laboratory pass over the smokehole. That would be very important to me."

"Look at this," said Anthony, lifting his weird left arm so she could see his loop.

"No," she said, and turned away. Anthony thrust the loop in front of her face. "So what?"

"Scratch it," he said. "With your fingernail."

She ran her fingernail over the curve of his forearm. Its substance came off in long flakes. "You're covered with wax," she said, withdrawing her hand.

"It's all wax," he said, breaking off a piece of thumb and holding it out for her.

"Jesus," she said.

"What's wrong?"

"First you get a foundation grant, then you're all made of wax. Jesus. What do I get?"

"What do you expect?"

"All I want is to see the skylab manned space station pass over the smokehole of my tipi. That's a simple request."

"Our tipi," he said.

"That's all I want."

"You'll see it," said Anthony. "I'll make sure you do." He lay back to look at the stars through the loop of his left arm. They heard the owl whooling in the ponderosa. The tipi glowed like an ember.

"I've got it," said Anthony.

"What?"

"The skylab. I've got it surrounded with my arm-loop. Come here."

"That's not the way I want to see it," she said.

"Suit yourself," he said. He looped his left arm over her leg and dragged her back into the tipi. Her mood had passed. She was giggling. Despite her feminist opinions she liked playing cavewoman. That night they made love with her on top because she didn't want to look through the smokehole until she knew she could see the skylab there. It was a warm night, and his body softened beneath her. She liked that. She pressed his shoulders flat. She left the impression of her nipples just under his chest. She shaped his penis into a spoon and finished herself.

II

Next morning Holly cooked the eggs. Anthony took off the tipi cover and they sat down to breakfast under the poles, just the dewcloth hanging like a fence at eye level around them.

"You see?" said Anthony. "I'm going to turn the tipi around so the smokehole faces more or less the orbit of skylab."

"We'll fill up with smoke if you do that. I'm happy as it is. I can watch Sagittarius rise."

"That's not enough. You should get to see just what you came here to see. Who knows when you'll have a tipi again. We just won't build a fire."

"Then I won't be able to stay," she said.

"Why not? You won't get cold."

"Sagittarius is my rising sign."

"You can wear my sweater. You can wear my jacket. You won't be cold," he said.

"Okay," she said, and they left the discussion uneasily resting there and settled down to the eggs. They were folded over as an omelette. He lifted the lip of the omelette and looked at the flecks and streaks that were cooked into it.

"What's in this omelette?" he asked.

"It's a forest floor omelette," she said. "It always jumps into the eggs by itself, so I incorporated it this time. It's good."

"It's dumb," he said.

"Cook your own breakfast tomorrow, and I bet you won't be able to do it without going to town for some bacon or ham. You won't be able to rough it. You'll want sausage."

"I'm not going to town just for bacon," he said.

As he sipped his second cup of coffee he heated his left leg by the fire and twisted it so the knee was turned backwards. He stood up on this arrangement. It seemed very stable.

"Hello."

Anthony wrapped an arm around Holly and responded tenderly, "Hello."

"Hi," said Holly, puzzled. She hadn't spoken first.

"Hello."

They both looked up. People had gathered around the dewcloth and were peering in at them. They were like puppets, heads and shoulders visible above the line of cloth.

"We're on a long hike," some of them said.

Suddenly Anthony and Holly felt very close to each other in the ring of their tipi in the middle of this audience in the middle of the woods. They held each other close. Their relationship at that moment was big and alive.

"We hike so very slowly."

"You caught us turning the tipi around," said Anthony. "That's why the cover is off."

"Not to be embarrassed. We didn't expect to see anyone at all. We do it so slowly."

"Well, come on in," said Holly. It was like suddenly inviting the audience into your act. Fourteen people entered their tipi, moving slowly, so slowly Anthony was intimidated, and went to work untying the dew-cloth so he could move the poles. Holly was fascinated by the utter slowness of the group, and kept up with them as best she could.

"How did you do that to your leg?" The leader of this hike, a man with a shaved head, asked Anthony. Anthony shrugged, no way to explain it. He showed the man how he could raise and lower himself like a scissor-jack.

"We haven't got to that yet," said the leader. "We're just into moving very slowly. Very slowly."

To Anthony that was very irritating. They tried to help him take down the poles, reset the tripod, put the poles back up; and whereas it might have taken half an hour with Holly's help, it took more than two hours moving at the hikers' pace, and it exhausted him having to restrain the poles as they slowly raised or lowered them. Holly was off with some women in a nearby clearing, learning their slow exercises. They told him they were headed North, to the lake at the end of the trail, which was three miles further on. For them it would be another seventeen days, but it was worth it. It would give them time to digest their food. They could float in the lake. Most of them, the leader told him, knew how to float.

"How did you happen to come here?" asked a young man who was trying to help him peg down the tipi cover. "I mean we're a club and we do it together and it's our thing. But how did you two get to do it alone? You must be exciting people."

The question stumped Anthony. He didn't know how or why, just that it pleased him to be here doing this. It felt good. the young man slowly slapped at a peg. It made no noise when he hit it. The peg wasn't going in. "I got a grant from a foundation so I could do it," Anthony finally said. "Somebody gave me a grant."

"How fascinating that is," said the young man, as his tent-peg fell over. He rose up slowly to follow his club that was slowly leaving. They moved among the trees like evening shadows. Anthony rushed around, driving in the rest of the pegs, and then headed the other way down the path. He needed a change. "I'll pick up some bacon in town," he shouted to Holly, as he was leaving.

Another telegram from the foundation was waiting for him in town. They assured him that if he only appeared and satisfied the members of the board that his project was feasible he would get the money. There were twenty-two thousand dollars. Anthony had never imagined that much money all at once. He could build a concrete poem. He could think about an immense piece of conceptual art. He could finish the research he hadn't yet begun on the underwater tipi. He could compose his piece for sixteen amplified sitars and latin percussion. He could write an endless novel about the Second World War. He could make a thousand hours of uninteresting videotape. He could conduct a statistical survey of the sociology of evenings at the airport. He could explore the possibility of draining Lake Erie into Hudson's Bay. He knew a lot of things he could do. He just didn't think he wanted to leave the woods. Questions rang in his ears. He pressed them down over the ear-holes, and they stuck themselves shut.

It was almost dark when he got back with the bacon. Holly was gone. He called her name, but no answer from the woods. She had probably left with that group of slow-movers. He had had a premonition that she would. They were out of sight, maybe a thousand feet up the trail by now. He wouldn't chase after her. Let her chase after herself at that pace. She would come back if she really wanted to.

He built a fire and cooked some bacon. It tasted really good. A small wind filled the tipi with smoke. He lay down on the bed under the smoke and dozed off. When he woke up the smoke had cleared. He peered through the smokehole, fondling her binoculars. Cassiopeia was visible. Suddenly he saw it, crossing the W: the skylab. It moved very quickly from one tipi pole to the next. It was small but spectacular. Holly had had the right idea. By the time he focussed the glasses, the manned satellite was gone. Skylab had just passed over the smokehole, and it made him feel very lonely.

III

A small black bear visited the camp two days later, and peered into the tipi where Anthony was sitting in what you might call a twisted double lotus position. He had wrapped his legs around each other twice and had rotated his trunk so his nose would have been in line with his backbone if he hadn't moved the nose to a new situation just above his right knee where he could scratch it without shifting his arm very much. He had been sitting in that position for eighteen hours. It troubled Anthony that he had noticed the bear. He certainly wasn't as far into the meditation as he had imagined if a small bear could distract him. "Welcome. Come in," he said to the bear. The creature entered as if it had understood. "This tipi belongs to me and Holly, but Holly doesn't live here any more." The bear stood on its hind legs and waved its slobbering head back and forth. It wasn't listening, not really. He had nothing more to say to it. As far as he was concerned the little bear was a big bore. It dropped to all fours, and headed out of the tipi for the food box. He tore the lid off, grabbed the ginger snaps and a jar of peanut butter, and ran for the woods. Let him have it, thought Anthony. He wasn't into it any more. He missed Holly and her goofy point of view. The woods wasn't the place where he could get himself together any more. It was time to leave. Rain was threatening. Everything was hungry in the wilderness, but nothing was really desperate. He wanted to go back to the city where everyone was desperate. He put back into shape all those parts of his body he had been experimenting with, closed the smoke flaps, and got out just as the downpour began. He left everything behind. If Holly ever came back she would have somewhere to stay. She had paid for half the tipi anyway.

"You probably can't figure it out, why I ripped your damned phone out, sucker." Anthony listened to his ex-friend, Larry, from a pay phone on the corner.

"Take it easy, Larry. It's okay."

"Six months at least was what you promised on that sublet, and you gave me three. I would have put it in writing if I knew you were going to be such a shit."

"I'm very sorry about that, Larry." Anthony noticed on his return to the city that New York immediately had a way of being New York.

"I've been setting up these chicks. That's why I ripped out your fucking phone. Why should you get the calls when things started to happen? Shit, I can't invite the kind of woman I've been meeting to the Chelsea Hotel. They'd freak completely at my roommate. That's why I ripped it out."

"I understand, Larry."

"And I sold your fucking furniture too."

"I noticed that. That's okay. I don't need it."

"I'm even sorry I forwarded your mail."

"I called to ask you to send me the mailbox key."

"I'll mail it to you," said Larry.

All Larry had left him was a busted wooden chair in the closet. Anthony split it into kindling and stacked it in the center of his room like a tipi fire, and he slept curled up on a mat by the unlit fire. He wouldn't ever want a bed again. If he could light a fire he would have the best of both city and country.

When Anthony finally met the mailman the key hadn't come, but he did give Anthony a registered letter from the foundation. They wanted to know if he intended to accept their grant on the condition that his interview was successful, or if they should dispose of the money in some other way. The members of the committee were anxious to meet him. They admired his work, and wanted to clear up just a few questions about the project he had proposed. The total of the grant was up to about forty-five thousand dollars. If he only could have remembered what the proposal was, Anthony would have rushed to the foundation office. It would have been too embarrassing to appear there with nothing to say. What had he proposed? If he had had the chance to be in his own shoes at the time what could he have come up with? He sat down to stare into his unlit fire. It didn't flicker. Tongues of flame didn't lick out at the ceiling. Smoke didn't burn his eyes. He didn't need to hunt for wood to keep the fire going. He stared into the unlit blaze and had no thoughts at all.

"Hello."

Holly was standing across the room from him, her face not glimmering with eerie shadows from the unlit fire. He had left the door open, because he figured there was nothing left to steal but an unlit fire. Holly's eyes didn't flash. Her teeth weren't glowing weirdly.

"Hello," Anthony responded, and he stood up. It felt peculiar to see her.

"I brought you the tipi. I thought I should give it to you." She seemed to hide in the motionless shadows. A tall black man carried in the bundle of canvas and threw it down in the center of the room. It snuffed the unlit fire.

"It's good to see you again," said Anthony. "I've thought

about you a lot, but I didn't know what to do."

"You did the right thing," she said as she stepped forward and took the arm of the tall black man. He was wearing an impeccably tailored double-breasted grey suit. "I thought about you too, the other day. That's when I decided it would be best to give you my share in the tipi."

"I still think of it as our tipi." He pulled the canvas aside and started to reset the fire.

Holly and her friend walked around in front of Anthony. "I want you to meet Aldrin Bean Carpenter. We're going to get married. He's a meteorologist and a Captain."

Anthony shook the man's hand and smiled. It was very civilized.

"He's going to be the first black astronaut. And he's going to take me with him."

"Do you want your binoculars back?"

"Of course not," she said. "I understand myself better now, and I understand you too, and what our relationship was. That's why I decided you should have the tipi. I want you to keep the binoculars too. You can lie back at night and watch me pass over your smokehole. I'll watch for the glow of your home from my skylab kitchen. I'll be your space-age angel, because deep inside I still love you." She moved even closer to her friend when she said that.

The black astronaut knelt down beside Anthony and helped him lay some sticks on the fire. He pulled out a small brass cylinder. "They gave us this new zero gravity pipe lighter, even though you can't smoke in the skylab. You can have it."

"Gravity is one-hundred percent in our tipi."

"This works anywhere," said the astronaut. He opened it and a long blue flame shot out, kindling the fire.

"Great," said Anthony.

"Holly told me you were made of wax. Is that true?"

"Sure," said Anthony. He warmed his arm over the fire and demonstrated its malleability. The astronaut shook his head in wonder. He'd seen a lot of amazing things in his program, but never anything like this.

The small fire crackled and popped, and flame cast a warm glow on their faces and in their hearts. The little smoke brought a tear to each eye. "I never really was really into tipis," said Holly, nostalgically. "And tipis was where it was at with you, Anthony. But as soon as I met Aldie here I knew I could get into skylabs in a big way. That's where my head was at all along."

"A fire is a wonderful thing," said the astronaut. "You watch it with a primitive part of yourself. It's irresistible. Cave life must have been cozy."

"Too bad you can't burn one on the skylab," said Anthony. He noticed that Holly's astronaut had become preoccupied with melting his elbow with the zero gravity pipelighter.

"Is this okay? I didn't even ask. I'm sorry," said the Captain. "It's my scientific curiosity."

"Go ahead. I'm tired of doing it to myself." They sat by the crackling fire in the middle of Anthony's bare-walled downtown apartment. This was an unusually relaxed evening in the city. Holly hummed very prettily some old Woodie Guthrie songs. The fire smoldered and smoked politely. Anthony found his own liquefaction to be utterly fascinating. He was developing into a nice puddle of wax near his apartment tipi fire. When Holly and her fiance left there were just a few embers glowing. Anthony's head, the chin spreading out into the rest of himself, was weeping nicely. It was a change of pace, to feel some sentiments. Holly returned just before they shut the door and kissed his forehead. "Listen, Anthony honey, if you ever come through Houston, that's where we'll be for a while. You be sure to stop in and see us, you hear." She kissed it again. "Ciao, Anthony."

Anthony admitted to himself that a whole phase of his life had ended.

IV

In a few days Anthony got himself together enough to make his appearance before the foundation committee. It was so very easy to get there that he felt foolish for not having done it sooner. The secretary showed him into a small, tastefully appointed office, one wall covered with prints by various artists who had received printmaking grants. The three members of the committee entered and shook his hand. The secretary brought in coffee and cookies. Everyone smiled at him as if he were someone special. It was as if they were too shy to broach the question of Anthony's project. Anthony was depending on necessity to be the mother of his invention, hoping it would come back to him once they asked about it.

The office hummed with amenities and air-conditioning. Anthony wished he could light a fire. When the secretary laid his folder on the table the committee gathered around it, looking from Anthony to his folder and back. Something wasn't right. The feeling changed from affability to consternation. One of them peered at the application through an illuminated magnifying glass.

"It's the same name," said the man with the crew-cut. "But the face is a different one."

Anthony looked at his face in a mirror, and then at the snapshot. He agreed with committee. They didn't even look to be by the same artist. The signature and handwriting were his, but he couldn't remember ever having seen the face in the photo. At some point he had totally goofed. Had it happened before or after he had turned to wax? Had he changed his looks so drastically?

"It's hard to know how to proceed. Were you playing a nice trick on us with this picture?" They all smiled at the possibility of a trick.

"Maybe it was a trick, but I didn't know I was playing it. I mean . . ." Anthony looked at his paint-spotted shoes tapping the blue rug. Now he wished he wasn't there. Now he wished he wasn't Anthony. He leaned back and closed his eyes. An image of the convergence of the tipi poles flashed against the inside of his eyelids, the smokehole open to some running clouds. "I guess I should explain." He looked at them all. For the first time he noticed the wicks, like topknots, growing out of their heads. "I . . . I discovered I was made of wax, you see. I don't know how to explain it, but that's what I'm made of . . . so that picture was me before I . . ."

The committee was laughing. He hadn't meant his confession to be funny. For the first time Anthony felt that this must be a dream, this bland torture that was turning into his life. "Some day you'll come over and have dinner with me and my wife," said a committee member. "You'll make her laugh."

This must be someone else's dream from which he wasn't free to wake up. The dream of a figure in a wax museum. It had been going on all his life. What if someone else woke up? The secretary entered with a lit cigarette lighter to announce that she was going out for lunch. She lit the wicks on each committeeman's head so he burned steadily as he laughed. Anthony had never thought of a wick for himself. What a simple idea.

"It's true," he said, and held out his arm. "All wax." He passed his arm over the flames of the committee. It was as if he had never felt pain before. A searing flash through his body. Agony. As if formed of the sum of all suffering he had ever been able to ignore. He jerked his arm back. A blister started to form. It was embarrassing. He was ready to confess.

"Spread some butter on it," said a committeeman.

"Vitamin E works better," said another.

"I guess he's not the person I think I am," said Anthony, and he got up to leave. "I guess I'm not the person I thought I was." There was an elevator waiting for him to descend. He was sorry he had ever left the woods. It might be snowing there by now, and he would be happy surviving. This had been the most confusing day of his life.

On the next day he received another letter from the foundation. They had deemed his project worthy and the committee had enthusiastically decided to award him the grant. Enclosed with the letter was his photograph stamped VOID and a check for eight thousand dollars. He would receive a check bimonthly for the tenure of his grant. Anthony held the check up to the window so the eight thousand and 00/100 dollars stood out like a shadow. The telephone rang. There was a tap on the window. Someone was knocking on his door. Anthony gripped the edge of the check as if he were hanging from the rim of a cliff. A siren sounded in the precipice. When he opened the newspaper he saw his picture. Most radio networks announced his name. His face appeared on television and he was grinning, and why not grin at this luck, at this beneficence. He let go of the check and let himself drop, floating into the space like a feather, like a leaf, like a page from a memo pad. The big check floated down beside him. He had certainly lived long enough to deserve this, though some people had lived longer and got zilch. He pulled the check into his lap and suddenly it came. Snow was falling on all the avenues of the art world. It was an idea about his project. It was midwinter everywhere, and he finally remembered the project he had in mind.

on
SELF-KNOWLEDGE

on
SELF-KNOWLEDGE

I have taken all my characteristics — my compulsive eating my
inability to make most decisions my fanatical mushroom hunts
my cooking with fingers crossed my occasional cruelty my irra-
tional flashes of temper my secret political awareness my nausea
when faced with bureaucracy my immobility on humid days my
don't take that pill mentality my overwhelming attacks of sheer
lechery my tendency to exaggerate some of my exploits the
gnawing below my heart when other writers seem to have more
success or more luck than I my apparent affability which I have
never believed in my indifference to the suffering of other people
my cynicism about my mother's situation my body's love for
heavy work my suspicion that other writers are geniuses my
knowledge that other writers are rich my fingering the change in
my pocket my mind's resistance to focus my love for books my
inability to remember the books I love my suspicion that any-
body is more wise more clear-headed than I my inability to fill
out the simplest form my dislike for games of cards chess
monopoly go checkers all that shit my preference to sit in a cafe
with a drink and gape at the people or watch the swallows if
they're flying my indifference to gossip my extreme pleasure at
eavesdropping on other people while they gossip my hatred for
doctors and hospitals my uncertainty about the writing I do
about the writing anyone does my joy at doing certain work that
breaks my back my resistance to finish little tasks my compulsive talking about money when I'm broke my compulsion to
spend all I've got my buys of vintage wine my Slivovitz my
Faville's London Dock Rum my Laphroaig Scotch my Rebel

Yell sour mash bourbon brewed exclusively for the deep south
my curried oatmeal my tofu in brown bean sauce my deep
involvement in the soft discipline of Tai Chi my thrilling thirty-
six hour fast each week my ears in Cape Breton my mouth in the
brook my eyes in the spruce my prick in the gulf the many things
I know my inability to dig in and know this well my continually
screwing up the facts of any issue my continually screwing as
decreasingly many women as I can bear my tendency to feel that
anything people do out of kindness cruelty despair loathing
talent loneliness joy greed pride ignorance certitude foolishness
etc. is interesting my lack of moral conviction my conviction
that I am totally moral my tendency to keep myself half hidden
my tendency to put on half a show my love for my ex-love for
my ex-wife my love for my kids my love for my feeling the
woman used me as a stud my beloved vasectomy my love for my
love for you my love for myself my inability to love anyone I
mean really love my tendency to wake up shouting Bateson is
right my love for my friends my feelings of guilt for much of the
above my feelings of stupidity for the same my feelings of pride
and anger and regret and doom and lust and optimism and grief
and anxiety and elation—all of this and anything I have ne-
glected to tell you I have compounded into these pills you see on
the table in front of you   you have come into my tent and now
you have swallowed the pill   its flavor is open to
interpretation   its affect will cure the monotony of these vis-
its   now I am here without myself as you see me   a spar-
row follows   some goose-tongue here
        this plastic cup   my tipi poles   come on with
        occasional blue   effortless the rain
I am the computer of doubt   I will lead you to the chanterelles
        we do fall among raspberries   hang on to this line
of sunlight   I am the twentieth century backing up
                I am the automatic transmission cutting out
            I have fastened my will to your molecules
the hands of these truths are formed of oystershells
closed on the moons of 1959

THE STOLEN STORIES

THE STOLEN STORIES

To say they swoop, or drift, or glide, would be imprecise. They don't plunge. These turkey-buzzards are called John-crows in Jamaica. That they ride the fabric of the air as it billows downward to the bay is too metaphorical. Down there the cruise ship with one blue stack brushed against its moorings. A, an American author, swirled the ice cubes through his rum and lime, and clipped the end off a good five-cent cigar. He sat with his back to Montego Bay and talked to B, another American writer who, with his son, Rafael, was a guest at the house where A was spending a year as a Guggenheim Fellow.

"Down here you can't keep the image of Errol Flynn himself separate from his role in the Captain Blood movie. To most Jamaicans, like George Huggins for instance, Errol Flynn is Captain Blood. The movie was even set in Jamaica. He, himself, behaved like he thought he was Captain Blood. He owned the biggest ranch around Port Antonio, that his widow lives on now . . ."

B imagined the tour buses pulling away from the ship to visit those duty-free shops to which the tourists had been guaranteed they would be transported, price of tour all-inclusive. One of the tourists, he imagined, was Emily Monthaven, from French Lick, Indiana, a youthful woman in her middle forties, who was travelling with her mother. Emily didn't prefer to travel this way, on packaged tours; in fact, she found it degrading. It made her feel juvenile, dependent, stupid; but her mother insisted on such tours, and while her mother lived it was her mother's money. Otherwise she wouldn't be able to travel at all. It was always her mother's money.

"Here's this story I told you I'd tell you about Flynn, that I heard through rumors and hearsay, but anyway it's a great story. He was partying on a yacht that a doctor friend of his had moored in the harbor. It was a long, drunk, decadent party. The doctor's son was visiting. He was a medical student at some big, northern medical school. It must have been a mess of debauchery on that yacht. Flynn had an enormous ego, and of course enough money to have things his own way. At a certain point in this marathon festivity they decided that since the doctor's son was studying to save lives he ought to first be initiated by seeing if he could take a life. They decided that he should kill a woman. They only had to figure out how to get someone to the ship whose life wouldn't be missed."

B still gazed at the ship below. "So decadent," he said to A, then he turned to his son. "Aren't you glad you're not one of those tourists being led around on that cruise ship?" Rafael watched a green lizard on the wall flick out the flap of orange skin at his neck to attract a female hidden somewhere. "I guess so," said the son. "But I've never been on one."

B imagined the heat on the poorly ventilated tourist bus made Emily Monthaven uncomfortable. She was not a hot weather person, but her mother had said Caribbean, and Caribbean it had to be. The bus stopped at a row of tacky modern tourist shops, their obsequious East Indian proprietors grinning in the doorways and rubbing their hands together. She needed a straw hat, and had to get some perfume for a friend, and her mother wanted a small silver chafing dish. She didn't know what for. When she reached into her purse to get the money her fingers played for a moment with the six bottles of valium she had managed to buy in Cape Haitian, where the drug stores sold everything over the counter. Just touching the bottles made her feel better.

Lisa, A's eight year old daughter, announced, as she came out on the terrace, that she was going to write a story. "Go ahead and write one," said A. "Can I use your pen?" she asked B. "Use your own pens and paper. Don't ask grown-ups for theirs," said her father. The late afternoon light was pink on the white limestone in the garden, and a thin spiral of pink smoke rose from the blue stack of the cruise ship.

"It was early in the morning when they made that decision," A went on. "Flynn went into town and woke up a certain man, a butcher he knew there, who frequently got women for him, sometimes young girls who needed money, sometimes prostitutes. He didn't tell the butcher how they were going to use the girl, but just that they wanted someone for the young man. The butcher got dressed and went out to look for someone."

"I want to take a swim," said Rafael. "Before it gets dark." He left through the living room. Lisa came back with a pad and pencil and took the seat Rafael had vacated, and stared at her empty page, and chewed on the eraser.

"I guess it was too late. The butcher couldn't find anyone in town. I guess all the young girls were in bed and all the prostitutes were occupied, so he woke up his own wife and convinced her to go to the ship and get the money. He took her out there to do what he thought was make love with the doctor's son, then returned to Port Antonio because it was time for him to open his shop."

"You got to know yourself, B," said George Huggins, as he came onto the terrace with a spliff smoking in his hand. "That's right." If you just measure him you might say that George is a slight man, but that isn't what you perceive when you look at him. His beard—the Rastas call a beard, 'stature'—gives his face magnitude, and his calm eloquence makes his presence quite grand. Prophecy is his preferred mode of speech, the Rasta mode. "Yes B, and A, I-n-I know a man for himself, for what he is. The man must know himself as well." George handed the spliff back to A and returned to the kitchen. B watched him go. It was a pleasure to watch people move through the open spaces of this tropical house, as if they were the figures that came through the openings of your own memory. He heard a splash as his son dived into the pool. The light was almost gone, only a very brief sunset in the tropics. Emily Monthaven had returned to her cabin where her mother seemed content to stay all day and look out through the porthole at the town of Montego Bay. The old woman smiled when her daughter unwrapped the chafing dish. "It's much too small for anything," said Celia Monthaven. "But you asked for a small one," her daughter replied. "I said small, not tiny." The mother, disgusted, looked back out the porthole. It was at times like these when Emily felt she could strangle her mother with her bare hands.

A drew on the spliff, held down the smoke, passed it to B. The marijuana was rolled in a piece of brown paper bag into a spliff about the size of a good five-cent cigar. B drew on it and coughed.

"I can't think of anything to write," Lisa whined at her father.

C, A's wife, came onto the terrace. "B, you should watch George cook the veg. It's beautiful. He's like a zenmaster when he cooks."

"You have to make it up," A instructed his daughter. "That's what writing a story means. You make it up." Lisa took this hint and started to write immediately.

B went to the kitchen. It was a pleasure to watch George Huggins do anything. The Rastafarian's belief, like the Zen Buddhist's, committed him to utter attention and devotion to whatever task was at hand. The focus is now, on what you are doing now, and through that love is manifested. "Yes, B," he said when B entered the kitchen. "I cook dem, B. Dem be Jamaican beans. I cook dem rice and use milk from dem dreadnaught, B." The beans and rice were mixed in a pot, and he was arranging some carrots, tomatoes and peppers to cook on top of them. It was beautiful, and strong. "I-tol, B. Heavy I-tol. Don't eat no pork. Yes, B."

C sat on the terrace now, in the seat B had vacated. Lisa tried to show A the story she had written, while he and C tried to discuss the use of their van for the next day. B sat down in the seat Lisa had vacated. "That's very good, Lisa," A said, after looking at her story. Cathy, their six-year-old, strolled onto the terrace and stared at B with superior knowledge. "You're not asleep," she said, continuing a private story that was going on between them. "Yes I am," he said. "Then why are your eyes open?" She put her fists to her hips and shook her curls, incredulous and gutsy as the original Shirley Temple.

"Tomorrow afternoon I'm going to see Jerry and I-ya," C explained to B. "It's a long trampoose into the bush. That's why I need the car."

"Jerry and I-ya?"

"I haven't told you about them. Jerry is a white Rasta queen, and I-ya is the man she lives with. He's a brujo, an Obie man, an herb doctor."

"How did you meet them?"

"When I think about it, it's such a strange one, I have trouble believing it myself," said C.

"I don't interfere there," said A. "It's totally her story, and her territory."

"I'll tell you," said C. "We were here last year for two months, and in the market I saw this woman selling veg. This was a white woman, and she had mighty dreadlocks; I mean, Mighty Dreadlocks." C showed the volume of hair with her hands. "And she was dressed like a Jamaican market woman, and was selling her veg with the others in the market, and she slept in the stalls with them overnight. It was very heavy to see her. I tried to talk with her then, but she wouldn't speak in English, only in thick patois. I understood a lot less patois then than I do now. And she was friendly, but she wanted to keep some distance. I got nowhere, but it was still mind-blowing to me. It's very heavy to see a white woman living like a black Jamaican, and not just a Jamaican, but a Rasta queen. I mean, that's unimaginable."

"Yes B, yes C, yes A," George Huggins sat down on the terrace with another big spliff he had just rolled. He lit it. "The veg is cooking, C." He passed the spliff to B. "You be in Jamaica, B. We open up your mind to the vibes here, to this space and time, in this cosmos." B passed the spliff to his son who had come in from swimming. "Ganja be good for you, B. Jah herb, Holy herb. It heavy, B."

"What else did you find out about her? Who is this woman? How did she get here?"

"Okay. I finally saw her again when we came back this year. She was selling her veg in the market and I talked to her again and this time she was very friendly. she invited me to her village, to visit her. I was very flattered. I knew I had to go there. Had to. No way I could stay away. But it took me a long time to get myself together to do it. And I needed George to come with me, just to mediate. No way I could go alone. They live in an I-tol village. I-tols are like Jesuits. They're the most orthodox of the Rastafari."

"I-tol very heavy, B. In troot and justice and Jah's name. I-n-I live in dem spirit, B. Live in dem spirit," said George.

"George and I finally did go out there."

"We trampoose, B. We go there."

"It's the first time I saw I-ya. He's one of those ageless older men — fifty-five, sixty-five. Jerry lives with him. She isn't thirty yet. We sat down together and she told me the story of how she got to live the life she did. How she got to Jamaica. She spoke in her heavy patois, only occasionally saying something in English for me. She's a total Rasta queen. There's no reason for her to speak English. That's why I didn't understand all of it, but I did get that she's from a middle-class Jewish family in Philadelphia. She was in college, and was always a very private person, but found herself becoming downright anti-social, depressed, withdrawn. She stayed in her room, saw no one for weeks at a time. This was a neurotic, middle-class girl. The family sent her to an analyst, to several analysts. Nothing helped. Finally the family withdrew her from school and sent her down to Florida for a rest, and she somehow went from there to Jamaica, to Negril, and one day with some people she knew she took a bus to Montego Bay. Those buses are really top-heavy, and they frequently turn over. This one did, and she was thrown into the bush, and was bruised a bit, but not bad. Well she was lying there in the bush, and from what I could understand there was this guy, these mighty dreadlocks, this Rastaman, just standing there, and he told her to follow him, and she followed him into the bush. And that's where she stayed. She disappeared. She lived for a year and a half by herself in a shack and spent that time learning I-tol cooking and herbs. And she really learned it; in fact, one thing we're doing is trying to write an I-tol cookbook together. Then she met I-ya, and spent several years trying to get him to live with her. Finally he did. You should see him. He's such a tiny man, and so black. I asked Jerry why she picked I-ya and she said, 'Look at him.' I-ya was busy, hopping around. His eyes were shining. He was smiling. He looked at you and you knew he was at peace. 'He's always like that. That's why.' Now she lives in this I-tol village, grows her veg, sells it in the market. She's a Rasta queen. She still paints, that's what she studied, and she tries to sell the paintings. They smoke herb all the time. It's so heavy, so far out. Sometimes I sit right there in front of her, talking with her, and I don't believe it's true."

"It's like some romantic fantasy," said B. "She has no problem that she's white?"

"No, B. No problem," said George Huggins. "Look at my skin. My skin is not black. I am not a pure African, B. One of my grandmothers was a Jewish woman, B. And I look at your skin, and I see it's not white. The British are white, but not you, B and A, and C. The Africans will return to Ethiopia, to our homeland, and you, B and A and C, you are the descendants of the original Arawak Indians, and you will come back to claim Jamaica, your native land. That is the prophecy. Yes, B."

"Arawak Indians?" B repeated.

"Yes, B."

"This Arawak is getting hungry," said A. "The veg must be ready." B went to the terrace rail, next to his son, and looked out at the cruise ship with its lights lit from stack to bow. "Arawak Indians," he said. "It's really pretty," said Rafael. Emily Monthaven and her mother must have been in the ship's dining room now, waiting for their dinner. They listened to the accordion, saxophone and drums. Celia Monthaven felt suddenly happy. The old woman got up and started to dance with herself, hugging herself around the dance floor. Old bag of bones, Emily thought. The fruit cup was on the table, and her mother was acting foolish. It was embarrassing, even though nobody paid attention. Her mother was easier to take when she was cranky.

"Do you want to read my story?" asked Lisa, as everyone started to go for the food. "Sure," said B. Lisa had reinvented a version of The Ugly Duckling, and had illustrated it. "That's a very good story," said B. "I know it," said Lisa.

That evening the two authors and Rafael went down the hill to the little store-pub in Anchovy, where the neighborhood people gathered to drink white rum, listen to the juke-box, dance, and play dominoes in the back room. A hung out down there with a group of men, mostly in their early thirties, who had all grown up together, and knew each other down to the bone. Gray, the furniture maker and upholsterer, was there, and so was Juke, a stone mason out of work, eternal optimist, always borrowing money, rarely paying it back. Juke is tall and powerfully built. That nick-name means slice or cut. It also means fuck. They say Juke does like to juke the women. Gray is a solid, witty man, whose small upholstery business makes him one of the few financially stable men among his friends. He lives alone, is a powerful player of dominoes, and lends Juke always less money than he asks for, but never expects it back. Benjy came in, looking glum. He is a waiter, out of work, who worries a lot about money. Since the election of Manley's socialist government, and the few over-publicized incidents of violence, the bottom fell out of the tourist industry in Jamaica, and work is hard to find. A hired Benjy to drive his kids to school every day, and that was his only steady income for the year. He also lent Juke one hundred dollars to have some cysts removed from under his eyelid, so he could pass the physical to go to work in the United States. The operation was postponed, and A suspected the money had vanished. "This is the way you turn a Guggenheim Grant into foreign aid," said A. Gurly is the clerk at the store, and the bartender. She borrowed fifty dollars from A to get a dress to wear to the Policeman's Ball. It was a red dress, and she had looked great. She had returned all the money but ten dollars of it she had lent to Juke, who has a polaroid camera, and had a scheme to make some money with ten dollars worth of film. "A good piece to write," said A, "would be to trace this Guggenheim money as it trickled down through the little town of Anchovy. That would be a nice story."

"This bar is one of the most relaxed places I've ever been," said B. "I feel privileged that I'm allowed to hang out with this bunch of friends," said A. "It's what I've always missed — a neighborhood bar, a bunch of guys to hang out with."

Gurley didn't feel good so she wasn't dancing, but Boy Campbell was dancing with his wife to the reggae on the juke-box. *Up Park Camp, It Sipple Out Deh, Woman Is Like a Shadow.* Boy is a handsome, powerful man, probably over fifty, but looking young. A says he looks like a king. *In A Dis A Time, Police And Thief, Jah Light Shining.* B danced with Mrs. Campbell, and everyone turned in his seat to watch, and applauded when they finished. "It's unusual for them," said A, "to see a white person loose enough to dance." White rum, 140 proof, simmered in the brain. "White rum is made for the black man," said Gray. "I don't drink no red rum." Everyone was dancing. "When they really get loose, sometimes late at night," said A, "they do a dance they call bondage. They start dancing as if chained up, their arms crossed, their bodies held in, and then they slowly pull the chains off. It's beautiful, and it tells the whole story."

"I was just beginning to feel loose enough to dance myself," said Rafael, as they started up the hill.

That night they went to sleep drunk in a flood of stories, each one gently kissing the margins of their lives, a limitless extent of stories cresting as far out as consciousness could reach.

"Come B, Rafael," said George Huggins as they got up early

next morning. "I show you my garden. I grow dem veg, B, and
Rafael. I be a heavy gardener." They followed George down to
the terraced garden below the house where cabbages and greens
and long beans were growing. The morning light was like a net
of gold over the green leaves. "Come. Now we trampoose down
to my other garden, my hidden garden. Now you really come to
know how heavy is George." They walked along the stone wall,
and then down some rotted logs to a small clearing below the
retaining wall, out of sight of the house and garden. In the
sunlight there, each in its own small hill, were some carefully
nurtured hemp plants. "This is my secret garden B and Rafael.
This be ganja. A don't know about this garden, B. Don't want to
know. That's how de mon is. A be a wizard, B. Only C know dis
garden, B. Heavy garden, B and Rafael." George kneeled
among the plants, and pointed at a particular one. "This be
Kaliweed, B. It female," said George. "Is that one Lamb's
Bread?" "No, B." He pointed out another plant with a more
downy, abundant bloom. "This one maybe grow to be the
Lamb's Bread. Dat be strong weed. Good weed." He moved on
his haunches to some scrawnier plants. "Dese be male plants,
B." He twisted the stem of one in his fingers till you would
expect it to break, then let it go so it slowly unwound. "Dem like
boys, B. Mon must twist dem, so dem become strong."

Lamb's bread is strong. You eat a brownie made with it and
time begins to open its gaps. "I feel like I'm living every moment
as if it's already the past," said A. "This is like instant nostalgia,
like I'm witnessing the narrative of the present."

After breakfast they took a ride up the coast, and at a certain
point began to drive past the huge landholding of John Connally. It went on forever: little estates, clubs by the ocean, pas-
turefuls of polo ponies, a lush golf course soaking up precious
water, a few neatly embalmed old white men in white pants
swinging golf clubs under the palm trees out of a scenario by
Scott Fitzgerald. A feeling of death was on this land, something
moribund conjured by the voodoo of American money. "When
they say Henry Kissinger is relaxing in the Caribbean, this is

what they mean," said A. "This is the money for foreign aid, and how it's earmarked for underdeveloped countries. It would be imprecise to call folks like John Connally buzzards. A buzzard wont eat living flesh, this one does." Connally's land goes on for miles, kept as green as money. "If Manley's government takes this one away from him he'll just lean back and tell his lackeys to find him another little country he can buy." Connally's Eagle's Nest in the tropics, for the Bebe Rebozos, the Abplanalps. A sty to house the super-rich, so disinherited, isolated with their money, immobilized, calcified in their accumulations. Jamaica entombed in this insidious, alien luxury.

"We shed a tear for dem," said C, as she took over the car for her trip to Jerry and I-ya."

By that evening the cruise ship with the blue stack was gone. B imagined Emily Monthaven steaming towards the Virgin Islands, or Trinidad, or home again where she knew that once and for all she would have to do something about her own life, and that meant doing something about her mother.

A stirred his rum and lime. "I still haven't finished that story about Errol Flynn." He stopped as C pulled in from the bush, and got up to meet her in the carport. Rafael sat down in the seat A had vacated, and helped Cathy read the text of a story from her picture book. Tess, the oldest daughter, almost thirteen, watched them from the living room. Lisa came up behind Rafael and hugged his head. "You're so nice," she said. "Oh, Lisa," said Tess. "Oh yeah," said Lisa. "A sixteen year old and an eight year old. Who would ever believe it?"

Something was wrong with C's tape recorder so they couldn't hear the choice conversation she had promised to bring back. "She talked about the cookbook and she said some things that if I heard them right are just amazing. Amazing."

"What things?"

"There was some stuff about excrement, about shit, that I didn't understand. Maybe I didn't want to. But it sounded very peculiar. And then, you know, we were talking about food, about eating, about I-tol cooking, and she was saying that it was better not to cook at all, that raw fruit was best. And I asked her what was the ultimate food, was there one thing you could eat, one basic thing, and she said, 'I-nana'. She would eat bananas. But she had to be ready for it, and she wasn't yet, but that was the ultimate: To eat nothing but bananas."

Early next morning B watched a John-crow perched on top of an electric pole. It waited for the sun to come over the hill and warm its wings. When the light hit, it stretched the wings, to dry them in the sun. The sun lit the bougainvillea, and the hummingbird sipping at the paw-paw near the pool, and the John-crow flew, sunlight under its wings. A emerged, and Tess, and Rafael, and the four of them drove off for Accompong.

Accompong is a Maroon village in a region of steep hills and narrow valleys called 'the cockpit'. The Maroons were escaped slaves who early in the seventeenth century, with the help of the Arawaks, began guerrilla warfare against the Spanish, and continued later against the British, ambushing them in the difficult terrain of the cockpit. They were invincible rebels, a big thorn in the colonial paw. Cudjoe, the founder of Accompong, was a great leader, courageous, a strategic genius. In 1738 he put his X to a treaty with the British that made the Maroons free and independent, the Maroon towns sovereign within Jamaica, and paradoxically the Maroons themselves were enlisted in the hunting down of fugitive slaves. "It's difficult to understand how they could do that," said A. B noted that in the banana plantation they were driving through the bunches were covered with blue plastic bags. "Cudjoe's story would make a great movie."

They stopped for a Dragon Stout and a Red Stripe beer on the way and several people recognized A from the last time he was through. A young man, carrying his beautiful year-old son, greeted A cheerfully. Another, who said he just got back from working in the States, ran to get his polaroid when he saw Tess. A man with a greying beard, a cloth fedora on his head, appeared in the doorway. "Oh, A, how nice, yes, to see you again. And your friends, oh yes, how nice in the vibes of dis place." Another Rastafarian, always recognizable by the rap.

"I-ray, Simit. How good to see you," said A. "This is Simit. A while ago I spent a lovely day with him, smoking and just talking and being with him. He's such a lovely man. His name is Smith. They say Simit."

"O yes. How nice. And now we have this time to be together in peace and love, and to talk and be and have good company. O my goodness."

"Doesn't he sound like Grady on Sanford and Son?" B asked Rafael.

"I knew he sounded familiar," said Rafael.

Simit continued on with them to Accompong. "Now I remember who that guy was," said A as he started the motor. "Who?" "That one with the kid. He's the guy who ripped off George Huggins' harvest. Now I remember. George, and a friend of his named Colley, had harvested a big crop of weed near Accompong. They expected the sale to set them up for a year. George was going to finish his house. They took turns guarding it, but one night Colley fell asleep outside the old mill where they'd hid it, and when he woke up the stuff was gone. George is sure that guy was involved in stealing it. You can see that he's kind of oily and ingratiating. I knew there was something I didn't like about him. They do that, steal from each other, some of them. George says that's what holds everyone back."

"His kid was sure beautiful," said B.

"Colley took the loss hard. He acted just like I would in his position. He tore his hair, berated himself; but not George. He just flowed with the loss. The thing happened. He let it pass. It could have meant a whole new room for his house, but he let it go. He's a high man, a totally remarkable man."

"I-n-I be good buddies. George me good friend. Oh yes, oh my goodness," said Simit.

There was an aura of 'state visit' around their arrival in Accompong. A was well known there, received like a foreign

dignitary. Colonel Martin Luther Wright welcomed them by
the porch of his blue stucco house, and in their honor ordered a
feast prepared of roast yellow yams. "But we have no salt fish,"
said his wife. "There's no salt fish anywhere," said the colonel.
"Yellow yam is best with salt fish, but it's good without it."
When A asked about the Maroon drum he had ordered the
colonel took him aside to ask how much he was going to pay.
"Thirty dollars," said A. "Let me get it for you. He'll only
charge me twenty-five," said the Colonel. They agreed to come
back for the yams and went on to George's house. He had gone
back to MoBay that morning to take care of a toothache, but his
wife was home. They entered the one small room where the
couple lived with six kids, to see the new baby. B understood
what the loss of the crop of weed had meant. They could have
more than doubled their living space. He also understood why
George spent so much time away from home, or with A. "You
know," said A, "George and I are like brothers. We have a very
intense exchange, and he also has an intellectual relationship
with C but for me his wife is like a shadow. I have never had a
conversation with her." They stood looking at the half finished
foundation of the unbuilt addition to the tiny house. A closed a
deal with one of George's sons for a black-billed parrot he
wanted to keep in his study, then they headed across town, up
the dirt main street, with its shacks, tin roofs pitched like the
roofs of miniature British country cottages, breadfruit and aki
trees, banana bush around them, past a small, sparsely stocked
store. As they walked they gathered a retinue of curious children
who followed them almost to the house of Mann O. Rowe. That
was who A really came to Accompong to see. He was an old
man, the unofficial historian and Secretary of State for Accompong. He was dressed in some old army clothes, a crushed felt
hat, his glasses slipped down his nose, the bottoms of the lenses
stuck to his cheeks with a film of sweat. A was surprised to see
him walking since he had been suffering from gout last time they
were together.

"You're walking good, but you still can't drink."

"I take a drink, A."

A sent for a flask of white rum as Mann Rowe arranged chairs around his table so all the men could sit in council. The old man's funky look belied his deep sense of decorum, and his innate dignity. He was proud of his own eminence as a literate man, and an historian. He layed a plastic folder on the table that contained the original document, of which he was keeper, of the 1738 treaty with the British. B read it clause by clause as they drank the white rum, and Mann Rowe talked. He braided an incredible rope of history, songs, superstitions, stories, quotes from Shakespeare. He was an herb doctor, and included some of that, and the children and women watched from the doorway, and A offered occasional official state advice on how to conduct Maroon affairs, and it was all punctuated by the musical incantations of Simit: "Yes. Dat be heavy monners, dat is troot. Troot. For dis we know, dat by de rivers of Babylon, where I lay down, and very well, remembered Zion . . ." And he went on saying the psalms according to Bob Marley.

The roast yams were laid out on the table at the Colonel's house, their aroma subtly sweet, their texture like packed snow. A paid the colonel for the drum, which Simit took in hand and immediately started to play. The young woman who had roasted the yams signalled B to follow her into the bedroom. He walked by a bulletin board full of pictures of the colonel in an oversized dress uniform, complete with epaulettes and medals. "Read this," said the young woman, and she handed him a note. "I love you and would like to correspond with you so hear is my address. P.S. give me your address. P.SS. Write me as early as you can." She was serious, stretched out on the bed, not smiling. "Do you want to take my picture?" she asked. "You can." She combed out her hair, put on a bright, flowered smock, and led B around to the back of the house. "Who's that?" asked A as she passed. "She's a good-looking young woman. Is that your daughter?" "My niece," said the Colonel. "There are three of them about the same age. Very difficult to find husbands for them these days."

"I'm really glad you were there," said A, as they drove back to Montego Bay. "When I'm there alone I get completely spaced, as if I'm in a movie or some fantasy. It's not a real world for me. Even though we didn't speak much, just eye-contact with someone from my own reality helps me to ground myself."

"That's what travelling, or living abroad is always like to me," said B. "It's living in someone else's story. You're moving on someone else's time."

"I'm in such a curious position with these people," said A. "I'm like a roving ambassador." Simit played the drum and sang in the back seat. The parrot squawked a few times, then settled in a corner of his cage. "Did I tell you that on New Year's Day I hired a van to take the leaders of Maroon Town to Accompong for their celebration. It was the first time they had met each other. Can you believe that? It was like my own shuttle diplomacy. The Maroons are in a unique position in Jamaica. They're like folk heroes, and you can't but think that if they could just get together they could exert an influence, if not on Jamaica as a whole, at least to improve their own conditions. They were really nervous about riding, because whenever they travel it's in an old car or truck that always breaks down. But I had rented a brand new VW van, and it was getting dark just as we were approaching Accompong, and they began to get really high, and to play their drums and sing these Maroon songs that were right out of Africa. I had a tape recorder going, but I haven't been able to listen to it yet. But coming down into Accompong as the sun was setting, the VW van full of chanting and singing, it was another world. I can't imagine ever writing about it."

When he got home A told C the following story: "Twenty-five dollars for the drum. Five dollars for the parrot. Ten dollars donation to the church. Five dollars to George's wife for the baby. A couple of flasks of rum . . ." The long story of the Fellowship dollars.

Some large bats flew in and out of the light on the terrace. Another cruise ship lit up, this one with two yellow stacks, brushed against its moorings. A swirled the ice cubes through his rum and lime, and clipped the end off a good five-cent cigar. His back was to Montego Bay, and he watched his kids watching T-V. Rafael sat down to read in the light of the terrace. Moths were called bats in Jamaica, and these bats that flew in and out after the insects attracted to the light they called ratbats. To say they flitted would be imprecise, and it was inexact to say they darted. They ratbatted around the edges of illumination.

"Do you ever save clippings from newspapers?" asked A.

"I use the newspaper sometimes," said B. "I write down phrases that strike me in the Chicago Tribune, for example, and see what configurations come up. It's all meat. Having stories to write keeps me alive. It's my psychic survival. I use anything."

"I have boxes of clippings that I pull things out of from time to time. It's useful; in fact, I don't use it enough."

"There are two stories from the South Bend newspaper that stick to me. One was about a sixty year old woman in England who tried to get her eighty-six year old mother to commit suicide on Mother's Day by convincing her to swallow a fatal dose of sleeping pills. The other went something like this – 'The mystery will never be solved, of the lion barely breathing found this morning in a drainage ditch in weakened condition, wrapped in a tattered blue blanket.' Those two stories seem to fit together for me. I don't know if I'll ever write them, but they seem to be copulating in my mind."

They could hear C talking to Juke in the kitchen. This was an evening of dominoes on the terrace and the boys were coming up the hill. "Before they get here let me try to finish that story about Errol Flynn," said A. "I was up to the butcher's wife on the yacht. Okay. The doctor's son kills the woman. That evening the butcher arrives at the yacht to retrieve his wife, and they present him with the body and tell him to dispose of it. Of course, no one there but himself knows it's his own wife, and he's too frightened and ashamed to say anything. He takes the body. The doctor's son goes back to medical school, prepared now to save lives. Errol Flynn and his friend continue their party. That is, anyway, the butcher's story, the testimony he gave at the trial."

"Do you believe it?"

"It's a great story, anyway."

Benjy and Gray carried a table onto the terrace. This game of dominoes isn't like the child's game. They play partners — Juke and A versus Benjy and Gray — and there's a lot of heavy intimidation and psyching out. "I be here to play heavy dominoes, A. I heavy. I heavy." Grey slammed a double three down at the end of the line. "Block." A was left without a move. "Ahhhhh," said Juke. "Dat be heavy monners, mon. Heavy monners. Me partner is strong," said Benjy. "You heavy, Gray," said A.

B finds a light in which to read the manuscript of A's new novel. He calls it THE PLUMBER. It's the story of a character named A who in the course of trying to dope out the nature of a complicated man, a plumber by trade, probably based on A's real father, he begins to know himself better. B was too distracted to read. He kept looking out at the lights of Montego Bay there in the lower galaxies. Emily Monthaven, he thought, was quite a bit closer to home now in French Lick, Indiana. They would surely be home on Mother's Day. Her mother had the custom of staying in her room on Mother's Day and expecting Emily to serve her. Although she wasn't as feeble as some people her age, her arthritis did make it difficult for her to move, and she was weaker than she had been just ten years back, when she could work in her garden all day. She really hadn't tasted a good zucchini or tomato since she had turned eighty and had to leave the gardening up to Emily. Even if she could move around fairly well, on Mother's Day she liked to be served. And she deserved it. She'd raised seven children, virtually by herself. Every mother deserved it. "These eggs," she shouted, and Emily rushed back into the room. "You'd think by now you'd have learned how many minutes it takes for a three minute egg. This is nearly hard-boiled."

Emily pushed a fork through her mother's egg. It was just right. "This isn't hard-boiled, mother."

"I hate to chew an egg, and you know that. I like to swallow it. An egg is like an oyster. But it has to be hot." She put the tray back in her daughter's hands. "And it's Mother's Day," she said as her daughter left the room. The door is slammed. "There should be some flowers on the tray. Some lilacs."

"Block, mon. Dat duppy you see last night warn you about dis? Heavy dominoes. Heavy." Gray had just made another strong move. Juke looked disgusted with himself. "Dat no duppy," said Benjy. "Dat a ratbat come to confuse dem dominoes."

B put down the manuscript and headed for the dining room where the parrot sat in its cage on the table. "You're not asleep," said Cathy as B passed in front of the T-V screen. "Yes I am." B put his chin in his hands and stared at the parrot. The parrot shifted from foot to foot and stared back.

Emily emptied the valium into a cup. There were about one-hundred and twenty capsules in all. She dissolved ten of them in her mother's fresh pot of tea. That would be a start. The timer rang at three minutes, and she rushed the eggs under the cold water, and then broke them into a small bowl. The toast was golden, just right. She buttered it and put a little saucer of marmalade on the tray next to the cup filled with valium. She wanted everything to be just right for her mother's last Mother's Day. She laid a fresh pink and red carnation between the toast and eggs.

"You know how much I hate carnations," said Celia Monthaven, smiling, obviously pleased. "They remind me of Edsel Pruitt. He always wore one when he came to see me, and you know what he was?" She squinted at her daughter. "He was a bounder." Emily pretended to pay no attention, but it bothered her every time her mother reminded her, as she had been doing since she was seventeen, that men rarely took notice of her.

Her mother lifted the cup of Valium. "What are these?"

"That's your arthritis medicine," said Emily.

"So much of it?"

"The doctor wants you to take a large dose for Mother's Day, so you can feel good enough to go to the auction."

"I have never gone to the Mother's Day auction, and I don't intend to now. They're a bunch of damned Baptists."

"We are Baptists too."

"I am a free thinker," said the mother. She took a sip of the tea and grimaced. "What's in this tea?"

"Mother, stop complaining. Happy Mother's Day."

"I think you're trying to poison me, with all these pills, and there's something in this tea."

"Mother, take your medicine. You're suffering from the delusions of old age. This is the doctor's prescription."

"It's Mother's Day, and my own daughter is trying to poison me. Tell me where I made my mistakes when I brought you all up." Celia Monthaven looked out her window, and at the dressing table next to it where the pictures of her dead husband and her murdered son were still draped in black. And the portrait of Haile Selassie, Lion of Judah, she had bought in Jamaica just on a whim, from that scary man with big beard and ringlets who came on the ship. The picture leaned against her mirror, and she liked it, the last really noble man who had alerted the world once to tyranny, so cruelly treated in the end, just like herself. Celia Monthaven actually began to cry. Emily left the room. The chips would fall where they could.

Dominoes was over, and Benjy sat down across the parrot cage from B and tried to play with the bird. He made small noises and stuck out his finger. "Dis bird still wild, B. Smart birds. When me was a boy, me trap dem." Benjy's delicate features were usually cast in anxiety and sadness, a persistent desperation from being out of work and poor in Jamaica, but he was clearly delighted with the little parrot, his brown face bright as a little boy's. "Dem very smart. Me trap dem in trees. Hit dem with rockstone and knock dem down. Den I tell you how smart dem be. Dey lie dere like dey was asleep, till you go to grab dem. Den dey grab you finger. Hurt you, B, den fly away. Smart birds. And dere be a woodpecker, B. You know him, pecks de wood. You go to grab it and it do dis." He pulled his lower

eyelids down with his index fingers. "Pull you eyes open. Peck you eyes. Really, B. Woodpeckers. Dem birds smart."
"You know it's damned hard to write fiction," said C, in the kitchen. "Especially if all you've ever written is poetry." When she was talking seriously C liked to settle on the kitchen counter with her legs folded under her. A poured a nightcap of rum over some ice and prepared to have this conversation again, that he'd had before.
"You've written about six pages. You can't know anything from that much writing. You have to get cracking," said A.
"You'll have to admit that it's damned difficult for me being married to you and trying to write fiction."
"This conversation again."
"I don't know why I stopped writing poetry. That's satisfying for me. I don't know why I told those people at Goddard that I'd agree to write fiction for this quarter."
"When you signed up for the Goddard writing program you knew why you were doing it," said A.
"Right. I want to get the certificate. I want a license."
"Stories are everywhere. It's all fiction," said B. "But writing it is hard, for anyone, for A, for myself," said B. There's even a story here, he thought.
"Then you have to go with the program or quit," said A.
"What I resent. I mean, I guess what I resent is that you have ten years of experience on me, A. You are ten years ahead."
"That is ridiculous. No one gets ahead."
"You are. I resent those ten years. You have to respect that."
The story is of husband and wife, of roles in marriage, of ambitions early and ambitions later, of woman's upheaval. The story of our times.
Early next morning they headed for Martha Brae, a small river outside of Falmouth, where tourists went to ride on bamboo rafts. They were going further upstream, to ride the rapids all the way down Martha Brae on inner tubes. No one but A and C's friend, George Butler, who was leading this expedition, had made the trip before. He had discovered the ride when he was a

boy, and his family would picnic on the river. He said it could be dangerous. George Butler is white, his family an aristocratic white Jamaican family, that along with other rich, and that means white, families, is trying to get its money out of the country around the severe restrictions imposed by the Manley government. His family is part of the white exodus. George Butler surveyed the river. "There's thirty percent less water than there was the last time I came down. I didn't realize it would be so dry. I came down in May before."

They plopped their tubes in the water, lay down on them on their backs, and slowly paddled downstream in the sluggish current. "Only George Butler would say that," said C drifting next to B. "Thirty percent less water. It's like a stock-market quotation."

"You know," said A. "George kept saying that Jamaica used to be wonderful, and it was probably going to get good again, so when C was riding through town with him she asked him what he meant. 'I'll show you,' he said, and he pointed at a pastry shop. 'You used to be able to get the best pastries there. And in that store,' he pointed somewhere else, 'the finest cloth from all over the world for almost nothing. And there, the most exquisite chairs.' That's what it means to him," said A. "For the privileged class virtue resides in good taste. They substitute taste for morality. Fitzgerald wasn't wrong. The rich live in their own reality."

The sun flashed through the dense foliage as they slowly floated down on their backs. High bamboo swayed and clattered in the wind, and dropped its bloom on the water that irritated the skin when they paddled through it. "The truth seems quite sinister when you think of the enormous piece of property that John Connally appropriated, or even when you think of that Errol Flynn story. Let me give you the rest of it." A and B floated side by side. This could have been Tahiti. This could have been South Vietnam. "The old guy who told me the story was actually the one who had discovered the body in the blue grotto. The butcher had been claiming that his wife was out of town visiting relatives. She had been gone for weeks. One day the old guy, he was a boy at the time, was fishing in the blue grotto, and he saw something under water. He dived for it and brought up a piece of a body. They found the rest of it here and there around the grotto. The whole thing turned out to be the butcher's wife. At first he denied knowing anything about it, but then he had to admit to it. The body wasn't just hacked up, but was expertly butchered at the joints, so it was obvious that he at least had disposed of it. The story I told you was the one he told in court. I think Flynn even testified. Of course the butcher took the rap, but it's hard to know what's true. I think it would make a great detective story."

"I love it," said B.

"I've even thought of using a detective from New Hampshire in it."

"That's a great story. I think I'll steal it from you."

"That would be great," said A. He laughed. "You could tell it to your rubber ducky." He paddled on ahead.

The shallow water made the ride more extreme. Either the current was sluggish and they had to pull themselves along, or the low water sped over the rapids and they got cut on the rocks. George Butler led C and some others around the shallow places through the grass where they picked up thousands of grass ticks on their legs. A, B and Rafael kept to the water, or the dry river-bed. They dropped down through some rapids that spun them around, ran them under a cliff, beat them against the rocks, and whipped them out through a whirlpool before it calmed down. A's back got slashed. B got cut up on his arms and legs, his bathing suit ripped open. "I feel like we're in a scene from DELIVERANCE," said Rafael as he spun by. He pointed to the sky where several John-crows were crossing back and forth. That adds a melodramatic touch to this story, B thought.

High up there those John-crows crossed the narrow band of sky that separated the bamboo growing on one bank of the river from the bananas growing on the other. That was putting it quite accurately. B leaned back on the slowly moving water and with a feeling of mild anxiety watched the configurations of buzzards and thought about Emily Monthaven, who waited for more than an hour before returning to her mother's room. Her mother was gone. She had drunk the tea, and at least half the valium had disappeared. Emily felt a thrill of nausea in her belly. If her mother really suspected she was being poisoned why had swallowed all of it? This was more like suicide, and that made Emily more like an accomplice. But where was her mother? She looked out the window for a sign of her under the maples or near the ornamental plum. One of the big bay windows was open. Her mother had probably climbed out. The sill was only three feet from the ground. Emily put on some clothes and ran outside. Their house was on about three acres that bordered a large woods. The old woman could be anywhere. Cars passed infrequently, especially on weekdays, so it was unlikely that anyone would have seen her. Emily felt as if she couldn't get air into her lungs, yet she thought they would explode. Her cotton smock was stuck to a film of sweat. "Mother," she called, very softly, as if she was afraid the old woman would hear and answer. She hid behind a corner of the house as a mailman pulled up to their box, left something, and pulled away. As Emily walked to the mailbox she thought she heard a moan. The mail was just an advertisement for a tour, this one to her liking, to the Pacific, the Galapagos, Easter Island, Tahiti. As she turned back to the house and looked up from the brochure she saw the figures lying in the culvert by the roadside. One of them was her mother. It was her mother resting in the embrace of a dwindling lion. The lion could scarcely breath, starved as it was, its rib-cage squeezed almost through its hide. The old woman pressed against its belly, her skirts lifted, her pelvis moving very slowly to the embarrassment of Emily. It was a mystery how it got there, this dying lion wrapped in a tattered blue blanket.

Three weird white males floating down the Martha Brae on inner tubes were observed with amazement and then with some amusement by some boys spear-fishing off the banks. They ran along the riverbank, waving their spear-guns and shouting obscenities in patois.

Around the bend the current picked up over some treacher-
ous shallow rapids. They could see C and George Butler waiting
at the cleared raft landing by the next bend in the river. A made
it down, and so did Rafael, but B's tube slipped from under him
and Rafael had to catch it downstream, and he had to cross the
rapids, ripping more flesh on the rocks. Six buzzards waited
there on a fence in the last patch of sunlight by the bank. That
his thigh and arms were bleeding made him feel like meat. He
was exhausted meat. He looked into the John-crow's eyes. A
curiously childlike shine to them. They were alert, but unimplic-
able. They watched him. He moved. To say they were wise
would be sentimental, just as to say 'ominous' or 'sinister'
would be melodramatic. These buzzards relaxed in the sun.
'Innocent' was the word that lay in his mind. Their red heads
bobbed a little on their red necks as they watched a bleeding
white man stumble from the rapids to the bank near their perch.
Even to say 'they are waiting' would be inaccurate. The author
hasn't yet become their meat. They have no role to play in his
story.

FICTION COLLECTIVE
Books in Print

Price List:

	cloth	paper
The Second Story Man by Mimi Albert	8.95	3.95
Althea by J.M. Alonso	11.95	4.95
Searching for Survivors by Russell Banks	7.95	3.95
Babble by Jonathan Baumbach	8.95	3.95
Chez Charlotte and Emily by Jonathan Baumbach	9.95	4.95
My Father More or Less by Jonathan Baumbach	11.95	5.95
Reruns by Jonathan Baumbach	7.95	3.95
Things in Place by Jerry Bumpus	8.95	3.95
Ø Null Set by George Chambers	8.95	3.95
The Winnebago Mysteries by Moira Crone	11.95	5.95
Amateur People by Andrée Connors	8.95	3.95
Take It or Leave It by Raymond Federman	11.95	4.95
Coming Close by B.H. Friedman	11.95	5.95
Museum by B.H. Friedman	7.95	3.95
Temporary Sanity by Thomas Glynn	8.95	3.95
Music for a Broken Piano by James Baker Hall	11.95	5.95
The Talking Room by Marianne Hauser	10.95	5.95
Holy Smoke by Fanny Howe	8.95	3.95
In the Middle of Nowhere by Fanny Howe	12.95	6.95
Mole's Pity by Harold Jaffe	8.95	3.95
Mourning Crazy Horse by Harold Jaffe	11.95	5.95
Moving Parts by Steve Katz	8.95	3.95
Stolen Stories by Steve Katz	12.95	6.95
Find Him! by Elaine Kraf	9.95	3.95
The Northwest Passage by Norman Lavers	12.95	6.95
I Smell Esther Williams by Mark Leyner	11.95	5.95
Emergency Exit by Clarence Major	9.95	4.95
Reflex and Bone Structure by Clarence Major	8.95	3.95
Four Roses in Three Acts by Franklin Mason	9.95	4.95
The Secret Table by Mark Mirsky	7.95	3.95
Encores for a Dilettante by Ursule Molinaro	8.95	3.95
Rope Dances by David Porush	8.95	3.95
The Broad Back of the Angel by Leon Rooke	9.95	3.95
The Common Wilderness by Michael Seide	16.95	—
The Comatose Kids by Seymour Simckes	8.95	3.95
Fat People by Carol Sturm Smith	8.95	3.95
The Hermetic Whore by Peter Spielberg	8.95	3.95
Twiddledum Twaddledum by Peter Spielberg	7.95	3.95
Long Talking Bad Conditions Blues by Ronald Sukenick	9.95	4.95
98.6 by Ronald Sukenick	7.95	3.95
Meningitis by Yuriy Tarnawasky	8.95	3.95
Agnes & Sally by Lewis Warsh	11.95	5.95
Heretical Songs by Curtis White	9.95	4.95
Statements 1	—	3.95
Statements 2	8.95	2.95

Flatiron Book Distributors Inc., 175 Fifth Avenue (Suite 814), NYC 10010